THE HOUSE OF WOOD

Anthony Price

House of Wood Publications

Copyright © 2020 Anthony Price

All rights reserved

The characters and events portrayed in this book are fictitious. Any similarity to real persons, living or dead, is coincidental and not intended by the author.

No part of this book may be reproduced, or stored in a retrieval system, or transmitted in any form or by any means, electronic, mechanical, photocopying, recording, or otherwise, without express written permission of the publisher.

*For
my family.
Love you all.*

CONTENTS

Title Page	1
Copyright	2
Dedication	3
Prologue	7
Chapter One	9
Chapter Two	17
Chapter Three	25
Chapter Four	36
Chapter Five	43
Chapter Six	51
Chapter Seven	60
Chapter Eight	66
Chapter Nine	72
Chapter Ten	82
Chapter Eleven	89
Chapter Twelve	98
Chapter Thirteen	105
Chapter Fourteen	112
Chapter Fifteen	120
Chapter Sixteen	130
Chapter Seventeen	137

Chapter Eighteen	144
Chapter Nineteen	155
Chapter Twenty	167
Chapter Twenty-One	178
Chapter Twenty-Two	188
Chapter Twenty-Three	196
Acknowledgement	203
About The Author	205

PROLOGUE

Silent it stood. The house of wood on the hill. Nothing surrounding it but fields. A vast, open expanse stretching as far as the eye could see. Ancient woodlands dotted the fields like pox marks. But, the house stood like a solitary statue, alone and foreboding. Its whitewashed wood shone out on the stark landscape like a beacon of despair. The only decoration was a single, dead oak tree in the front garden. A child's swing hung limply from a lifeless branch. No one lived there anymore. They hadn't for years. Without love and care the building had fallen into disrepair. Now, only the blackbirds were brave enough to land nearby. Usually, nothing stirred, except the swing blowing in the cold breeze. But not today. Two shadows danced across the window.

"Why are you doing this to me?"

"Come on, it's fun."

"Please, I can help you. Just let me go."

"I don't need help," the standing shadow snarled. Its hand whipped out, landing with a sharp snap across the face of the battered and bruised victim tied to the chair. "No one can help me."

The victim stared at the attacker. There was no way out. The rope bit the flesh of their wrists as they tried to twist free. Pain filled them. Tears welled in their eyes.

"Awww, poor baby. Here, let me wipe your eyes." A piercing scream filled the night air, as fingers jammed in to the sockets. "All better now?"

"I just want to go home," the victim sobbed, all hope evaporating. "Please, let me go."

"You're not leaving me. You're *never* leaving me." A perverse smile stretched across the attacker's face. "We're meant to be, you know that, sugar pie."

"I-I-I don't know what you're talking about."

"But you love me. You always have."

"No I don't, you're deluded and you need help."

"There you go again, denying your feelings. Well I know how to cure that."

The attacker's shadow slid across the living room floor, stopping at the open fireplace. Flames swayed like Egyptian belly dancers, hypnotic and seductive. The face of McCain in the portrait over the mantel stared out.

"What're you doing? Look, someone will come up here and stop you. Let me go now and you can escape, I won't send the police."

"Now, now sugar pie, I got a surprise for you." The attacker turned towards the victim. "You'll like this."

A petrified scream filled the night air. A young girl stood silently by her swing, watching the couple, a dark red stain across her beautiful white dress. She turned away, her expressionless face looking out over the desolate hillside. She sat down on her swing, and listened to the agonising screams emerging from the house.

CHAPTER ONE

Sunlight shone down through the narrow windows of the lecture theatre, and dust mites twinkled like stars as they carried out their playful dance around the room. All that could be heard was the monotonous droning of the professor and the occasional yawn from a student. Sullen faces dotted the seating area, some chewing gum, others slowly drooping into slumber. The ticking of the clock seemed louder and more ominous in the cavernous room. It was typical for a Friday afternoon lecture.

Rachel James' pen scratched away at her notepad, trying to keep up with the professor who was speaking at a million kilometres an hour. She had to get these notes down if she ever wanted to pass her mid-terms. So far she was flunking. A failure on this next test would spell her doom. She'd be out. And that meant going home.

"Okay class," the professor said, leaning across the front of his desk. "I know how you all love exams, so I'm going to set you a pop quiz for next Tuesday."

A chorus of groans erupted from the students, all of them knowing that their weekend plans were now dashed. Not that it bothered Rachel. She didn't have any. There was hardly ever a weekend that went by where she did. She wasn't a drink-until-you-puke kind of girl.

"I know, I know, I've heard it all before."

The bell rang out above Rachel's head, making her jump.

"Okay, that's it for today. Read chapters fifteen through twenty for the test next week." The professor gave them a sinister smile. He was enjoying himself. "Have fun this weekend."

Rachel finished scribbling down the last notes. It was as if she were invisible; people just walked past her without paying any attention, or even acknowledging her existence. Every now and then, someone would swing around too sharply and bash her in the head with a rucksack. She may as well have been a ghost.

She slung her things in to her own bag and stood up to leave. All she wanted to do was get out of the stuffy room and get back to her dorm.

"Rachel," the professor called from behind his desk. "Can you come here for a second?"

Great, that's all I need, she thought. She threw her bag over her shoulder and walked down the steps towards the front of the class. The professor ignored her for several moments while he tidied up his desk.

"You do know you're failing, don't you Rachel?" he asked, without looking up.

"Yes."

"And you do know that you need to pass this next exam, in order to remain on my course?"

"Yes, professor." She knew what was coming. This wasn't the first time.

He stopped and looked at her. His eyes roved over her, undressing her in his mind. He licked his hand and greased back his grey hair. "I can guarantee you that A if…"

Rachel didn't know what to say. Even though this moment had been building up for a while, a look here, a comment there, it had still taken her by surprise. She watched him as he stepped closer. Her blood was beginning to boil. Why do men think they can intimidate women like this? She fumed.

"What?"

She leaned in, licking her lips and fluttering her eyelids.

"I could make life so easy for you. Come on, tell me what you think?"

"I think," she said, "That you're a dirty old man, who has tried this far too often."

A loud crack echoed around the room, as her hand swung

out and slapped him in the face, leaving a large red hand print on a stunned cheek. He staggered back a step.

"How dare you think you can intimidate me," she screamed at him. "It's men like you that make women feel as though it's not safe for them to go out at night. You disgusting little pervert."

"Y-y-you can't hit a teacher. I'll have you thrown out."

"I couldn't give a damn what you do." She leaned in close to his face, fire burning in her eyes. "And I will be getting that A."

With that she left, slamming the heavy double doors behind her. She learned a long time ago to not let anybody get the better of her. She'd been through too much in her life already. The last thing she was going to do was bow down to some old has-been.

She strolled across the quad, dodging footballs and frisbees flying through the unseasonably warm October air, as throngs of people enjoyed the brilliant sunshine. There were far too many for her liking.

Tucking her books under her arm, she checked the time on her watch. She was going to be late getting to the campus library. It wasn't far from the lecture theatre, but the time she spent walking there was time wasted. She should have been heading back to her dorm to study, instead of meeting a friend. The words of her professor echoed in her ears. There was no way on God's earth she could afford to get kicked out of college. She wasn't going to end up back home.

Her steps quickened, as the sun dipped behind white clouds. She kept her eyes fixed to the floor, avoiding eye contact with anybody. At times she wished she could just disappear. Rachel hated being around crowds; the mass of students on the quad was like her worst nightmare. In a way though, she felt jealous. She didn't have lots of friends to just hang out with in the sun, or go partying with every weekend. Except for a couple of the girls in her dorm, there was no one. She couldn't connect with people anymore. She was too afraid of what they might do to her.

It didn't take her as long as she thought it would to reach the library. It was a tall building that loomed large over the surrounding area, casting long shadows across the street. The sides of it were surrounded by huge glass windows that reflected during the day, but allowed curious eyes to look in after dark. It featured a café; two garden terraces, one with views over the city; and an atrium. The long, winding staircase coiled its way upwards like a snake in the centre of the lobby. Students dashed to and fro across wide bridges connecting the never ending lines of dusty books, hurrying to meet their deadlines. There was hardly ever anyone up top, which is why she didn't mind it. She knew her friend would be up there.

As she reached the top step, a short blonde girl came bouncing towards her.

"Hey, I wondered where you got to," Becky Sawyer said, "It wasn't that sleaze-ball Professor Hoganstein holding you up again was it?"

"As a matter of fact it was."

"Oh my God, what're you going to do about it?"

"Nothing. There isn't a lot I can do."

Becky looked at her sternly. "Of course there is. For starters, you can go to the cops and report him. You could get him fired. It's no more than he deserves."

Rachel knew she was right. Becky was always right. This was at least the second time he had tried it on with a student. Last time, the girl ended up leaving and he got away with it. Some even said she was pregnant.

"What can I do? The police won't do anything without me being able to prove it beyond reasonable doubt and the College Board will be the same. They'll interview him, but he'll just lie and make it worse for me."

"Surely it's worth a shot?"

"No, I think it'll be best if I just leave it. I need to concentrate on my studies. Something like that will be distracting and I can do without it. Men like him always come out on top. It's the way of the world."

"Well I think you're stupid. What if it gets more serious next time? Or he tries it on with someone else who isn't as strong as you?"

"I don't know. I guess we'll just have to hope it doesn't. Now can we change the subject, please?"

Her friend said nothing, as the two of them went to find a quiet corner in the library café. It wasn't hard to find; the entire place was virtually empty, which was a surprise, considering the mid-terms were fast approaching.

The two of them had been friends since the first day of college three years ago. At that time they had been in separate rooms, but were in a lot of the same classes together. They had seemed to gel and were inseparable now.

She listened, as Becky chatted away about nothing in particular, and Rachel nodded and disagreed in the right places. It's funny how two people that are completely different can get along so well, she thought. Becky was a talker and a people person, but Rachel liked that about her. It reminded her of a friend she once had back home. Becky was her best friend and she'd be lost without her. If it wasn't for her, Rachel realised, she probably never would have made it this far. In all honesty, it was amazing she had made it to college at all.

"So are you coming tonight or not?"

The question snapped Rachel back to the present. She had been thinking about home, but couldn't remember why. It wasn't something she did often.

"Are you okay, Rachy-Bear? You look pale."

"Yeah, sorry I just switched off for a minute. What were you saying?"

"You've been doing that a lot lately. I wish you would go to the doctors about it." She sipped at her coffee. "Anyway, I was just saying that Ritchie and the guys over at Sigma Nu are having a party tonight. It's going to be wild. Do you want to come?"

"No I don't think so," Rachel replied.

"Why not? You always lock yourself away in that dorm room of ours."

"I had a wild night out once before. It didn't go too well."

Becky took Rachel's hand in her own. "You've got to stop living in the past. It's not healthy for you to keep dwelling on that. I know you went through a lot, but we've only got one year of college left and you *have* to start enjoying it, or you'll regret it for the rest of your life."

Rachel sat for a moment. Part of her wanted to go, but she couldn't bring herself to say yes.

"No, I think I'll stay at home. I've got way too much work to get done, before these damn exams start."

"It won't be the same without you."

"Sorry."

The two of them sat in the café for another forty-five minutes talking about mundane things. Clouds had begun to gather outside, casting a gloomy shroud over the city. Rachel's body was there, but her mind was elsewhere. She didn't know why, but something wasn't right. She put it down to the stress of being harassed by her professor and the approaching test which could seal her fate.

She stared out of the window. Something wasn't right.

***

Day had long crept in to night over the campus. It was empty, like a hollow shell. The excitement was elsewhere. On campus it was just dark, the students either hidden away in their rooms studying, or out spewing their guts up after too much alcohol. The night seemed heavy and oppressive; a black veil over what had been a bright autumnal day.

Rachel sat in the room, studying hard for her exam. Her eyes poured over the textbooks and notes that she had made, seeing, but not understanding. To her they may as well have been hieroglyphs from an ancient land. She kept looking at the Hello Kitty clock hanging on the far wall. It was one o' clock in the morning. Late. But not too late for a student party, she guessed. Although Becky usually rang if she was going to be out past midnight. Where was she?

She closed the textbook with a dull thud and sat up on the

bed. All day long she had felt something. Something wrong. She just couldn't put her finger on it.

Sliding off the bed, she made her way over to the window and looked out at the night. She hated the dark. Everything about it was alien to her. Remorseless and unforgiving. It hadn't always been that way. The same as she hadn't always avoided contact with people, or stopped them from getting too close to her. She wasn't even sure if she would be able to forget her past. It had played on her mind relentlessly for the last week or so, dragging her back to the horror. She had woken up several times, drenched in icy cold sweat, screaming out a single name. Justin. Why it was happening to her now, she had no idea. All she knew was she would never go back to Willows Peak.

She walked over to the front door, checking the bolt and extra locks were shut tight. The soft sounds of music filtered through the wall. The students in the next room were probably at it again. Rachel had become accustomed to their sexual habits, as they always played the same songs; a soft rock ballad, or Barry White. In a way, it made her jealous. She wanted to be able to feel the embrace of a man, the ecstasy of making love. She had tried, but when it actually came to the crunch, she closed up like a coffin. Never to be opened again.

As she made her way to the bed, the shrill ringing of the telephone filled her ears. No doubt Becky saying she wouldn't be home tonight, Rachel thought. She bent over and picked up the receiver. It was a man's voice.

Behind her there was a bang at the door.

"Hey, let me in."

Rachel wandered over, her body on autopilot, as she opened it.

Becky entered, a curious look on her face, as if she was wondering the same thing as her friend. *Who the hell would be calling at this hour?*

Holding the telephone to her ear, Rachel's eyes fixed on her room-mate, widening with every second.

"Okay, thank you," she said, placing the receiver back on

the base.

Suddenly, her knees buckled beneath her and she slumped to the floor, bile burning her mouth and throat.

"Oh my God, Rachel, are you okay?"

For a second she didn't know where she was. She couldn't breathe. The room span. She felt Becky pulling her up on to the bed.

"What's wrong?"

Rachel took a deep breath to try and calm herself.

"M-m-my parents," she started. Tears welled in her eyes. "T-they're dead."

CHAPTER TWO

"This place looks really creepy, Rachy-Bear," Becky said, glancing out of the passenger window.

"Welcome to Willows Peak."

The two friends, in a black Ford Focus, sped down the old dirt track, twisting and turning along the road. The dust cloud spewed from the Continental tyres like a mushroom cloud, out of the back of the vehicle. The road was ancient. It carved its way through the forest surrounding the hillside like a scar on flesh. The trees stood tall, next to the track like age old sentries. Their limbs hung over the road like frightening hands, as if they were waiting to snatch anything that came within their grasp. Every now and then, a flock of blackbirds would soar in to the sky, their dark silhouettes standing out from the grey above. They rushed to get out of the tight confines of the woodland, wanting to get away. It was as if they knew something the unwary newcomers didn't.

Rachel fixed her eyes on the twisted road stretching out in front of them. This was the last place in the world she wanted to be. Not after what happened the last time.

"Are you alright?" Becky asked. "You've barely said two words all afternoon."

"I'm fine." Rachel wiped her hand across her eyes. "Just tired, that's all."

"Okay, well do you want me to take over driving for a while?"

"No, it's alright. Besides, you don't know the way and we're not far now."

"Where are we anyway? All I can see are the trees."

"We're in the woods just outside," Rachel answered, her

gaze fixed to the road in front, but seeing nothing in particular. "We'll be there in about twenty minutes."

"Good, it'll be nice to get out and stretch. It seems to have taken forever to get here."

Rachel didn't answer. There was nothing nice about this place, she thought, trying hard to suppress her urge to swing the car around and get as far away as possible. They would be going past the hill soon; she could feel it looming in the distance. Her only small mercy was that she wouldn't have to see *it* standing there.

"You know, it's okay to grieve Rach," Becky said, turning to her friend with a sympathetic smile. "I'm here for you if you want to talk."

"What? Oh yeah. Thanks, but I'm okay."

"They were your parents. You're allowed to be upset."

"I know, but I'm fine. Honestly, I am."

"If it's not that, what's wrong?"

What's wrong? Everything is wrong, she thought, biting her bottom lip. She didn't want to talk, why couldn't people understand that?

"Nobody can criticise you for being upset about losing loved ones." Becky continued, putting her hand on Rachel's shoulder. "I'm worried about you Rachy-Bear."

"Don't be."

"I'm your best friend. I don't know why you can't talk to me."

Silence.

"Please talk to -"

"It's this damn place alright," Rachel snapped, causing Becky to jump in her seat. "I hate it. Nothing good can come out of being back here, nothing." She slammed her hand down hard on the steering wheel, sobs tumbling from here in frustrated bursts.

"Hey it's alright, I'm here with you. We'll get the funeral out the way, then we'll head back to college."

"It's not that simple."

The car swerved in and out of the lane. It had picked up speed. Tears burned Rachel's eyes.

"Slow down, Rach."

"I haven't even got my family anymore." The words fell from her. "I miss them so much. I didn't even get to say goodbye. I've got nothing left."

"You've got me, just slow down before we crash."

The words seemed to sink in. Within a few seconds, the car was back in the correct lane, cruising along the deserted road.

"Thank you, I'm sorry." Rachel wiped her cheeks with the back of her hand. "It's not easy for me to come back here. I don't have many good memories about this place."

"You want to talk about them?"

"I'd rather not."

Becky didn't push the subject any harder. For a time, the only sound in the car was the dull hum of the engine and the occasional thud, as the tyre hit a crevice in the road. The sun was slowly dipping below the horizon. It would be dark by the time they got to the bed and breakfast in town, Rachel realised. She just hoped no one would recognise her, even though she hadn't changed much in the three years since she had left. The scars were a constant reminder of that.

"Have the police said much about the fire?" Becky asked.

Again with the questions. "No not really. They think it might have been faulty wiring, but they're still investigating."

"But it happened weeks ago."

"Willows Peak is a small town. Things move slowly here. Anyway, can we drop it?"

"Sure."

Again there was silence. The trees along the roadside were beginning to thin out and the road had started to climb upwards. Rachel's heart thundered in the prison of her chest. Her breath came in rapid bursts. Thank God it was gone, she thought, as the car broke out of the trees. She had no idea if she could cope with seeing it right now. She took a deep breath and closed her eyes. As the car reached the top of the hill, she could feel her pulse slowing. Her eyes opened.

"No, no it can't be."

"What is it, Rach?" Becky asked, her voice full of concern at the sudden outburst.

"It's here, it can't be, it's not possible."

The words fell from Rachel's lips in an incoherent torrent, as the car started to swerve across the road again.

"Whoa, calm down, or you're going to kill us."

The car continued to thunder along, the speedometer needle indicating an ever increasing speed. They swerved in and out of the lane, the tyres screeching as they struggled to find purchase on the slippery tarmac. A horn blared out.

"Jesus Christ," Becky screamed, bracing herself.

A pick-up was coming in the opposite direction. But Rachel didn't care. It didn't matter anymore. She'd rather die.

"Rach, get a grip!"

Her friend's terrified voice broke through, just as the truck skidded around in a cloud of dust.

At the foot of the hill, Rachel slammed on the brake and jumped out as it skidded to a halt. She ran straight for the nearby bushes. After ten minutes of puking, she heard Becky's footsteps approaching.

"What the hell happened, Rach? What's wrong?"

"It shouldn't be here," Rachel said, rocking back and forth on her heels. "It was all gone, how is it back? It's not possible."

She felt Becky's hands yank her up right.

"Rachel, what's back? What are you talking about?"

"I can't, I can't. It's not real."

"You almost killed us back there," Becky shouted, shaking her friend by the shoulders. "I think I deserve some answers."

"The house of wood, up there on the hill."

Rachel couldn't fight back the tears any longer. Her sob riddled body collapsed in to her friend's arms. Her mind racing with questions.

"It'll be okay, I'm with you," Becky soothed, her own fear subsiding. "Let's get to town. I'll drive this time. I'm sure I can find it from here."

Rachel allowed herself to be led back to the car. She took one last look at the house before ducking down in to the passenger seat. Its black lifeless eyes stared back at her. Watching. Mocking.

***

Neither of them had said a word since the incident on the road. Rachel had just sat in the passenger seat, watching the world blur past the window. Every now and then a familiar landmark or building would fall in her eye line, stirring her back to life. She couldn't believe the house had survived. As hard as she tried, there was no pushing the old forlorn building from her thoughts. It was a mistake to come home, she realised, but there had been no avoiding it; she was an only child, so it was down to her to sort out the funeral arrangements. They were her parents after all.

Becky had been brilliant since the incident, not asking questions, or losing her temper. Rachel realised she had a good friend sitting next to her and she owed her a proper explanation for her actions at least. But how could she explain the impossible?

"Are you cold?" Becky asked. "I can put the heater on."

Rachel hadn't even realised she was shivering. She smiled. "No thanks, I'll be fine. The bed and breakfast is only a little further down the road."

Within five minutes, the black Ford Focus pulled up in the gravel courtyard of the only bed and breakfast in Willows Peak. Raindrops gently fell from the dense grey clouds blanketing the moon. Becky hopped out the car and began unloading the trunk.

"You going to help, or are you sleeping in the car tonight?"

"Gimme a sec, okay?" Rachel replied.

She needed to get her thoughts in order before facing the

next few days. So what if people recognised her? It wasn't as if she had done anything wrong; she was the victim in it all. At the funeral, familiar faces would be unavoidable. It had all happened three years ago and the past couldn't hurt her now, she reminded herself. *But the damn house.* She couldn't shift the sense of dread she felt at seeing it standing there, as if nothing had happened.

A tap on the window shattered her reverie. Becky's face beamed back at her.

"Come on Rachy-Bear, let's get inside."

Rachel followed her friend up the few brick steps and into the quaint little building.

Stepping inside was like going back in time. The reception room looked like a movie set for a 1930s film, with its yellow walls, oak staircase and black and white photos dotted sporadically around the walls. Along one wall was a dresser, covered in a beautiful lace doily. On top sat a blue vase with a bunch of perfect, white lilies.

A little old lady shuffled in from the living room. "Can I help you girls?"

"We're looking for a room, if you have one?" Becky informed her. Rachel stood quiet, not wanting to draw any of the woman's ice cold attention.

Mrs Ryan glared at the two girls, squinting as she did so. "I only have the one room and it's one-hundred and twenty dollars per night."

"What? That's way too steep."

"I'll give you a ten percent weekly discount. Take it, or leave it?"

Becky turned to Rachel. "What do you think we should do? There must be somewhere else we can stay?"

"There isn't. The nearest town is Merryville, but even that's miles out. It's this, or the car."

"So, you'll be wanting the room then?"

"Yes please," Rachel replied.

Mrs Ryan smirked. "I'll fetch the key. Wait here."

She shuffled back off in the direction of the living room. Rachel felt like she had been in a blender. It had been a rough day and all she wanted to do was go to sleep; she could do without the old dragon making things difficult for them.

After a few moments, Mrs Ryan returned. "Here we go. It's room three, straight up the stairs and to the left."

Becky took the key and started to make her way up the wooden staircase. Rachel followed close behind. She had made it up three steps, when she felt a tug on her wrist.

"I know your face," Mrs Ryan declared, looking in to Rachel's eyes. "Are you from around here?"

"Y-y-yes, I am. I lived on the other side of town. Long time ago now."

"I see. There was a fire over there a short while ago. Nasty business. The papers say it was arson."

"Well, don't believe everything you read," Becky snapped, pulling Rachel's other arm.

"Wait, I know who you are now." Mrs Ryan let go of Rachel's wrist as if she might catch some awful disease. "You're the young girl from the news a few years back. You had some trouble out at the old farmhouse. Now I don't want any nonsense from you two while you're under my roof. Is that under -"

"Look, I don't mean to be rude," Becky cut in. "But we're tired after a long drive. So, if you don't mind, we'll be going now. Come on, Rach."

The two girls left Mrs Ryan to watch them with disdain, as they made their way to room three. Becky closed the door gently behind them.

"God that witch is awful. Are you alright?"

"Yeah I'm okay, just tired," Rachel replied.

"I'm really sorry, but I have to ask, what happened to you here? Does it have something to do with that creepy old house? I've never seen you so afraid before."

"I'm sorry, Becky, but I'm really tired and would rather not get in to it right now. All I want to do is avoid any more drama and get in to bed."

"Okay, but only if I get the left side."

Rachel feigned laughter. Her mind was several miles outside of town, as she undressed and got under the covers.

"Night, Rachy-Bear."

"Goodnight."

Her mind was still at the house long after she had fallen in to a fitful slumber, full of spectres from a past she had long suppressed.

CHAPTER THREE

"We therefore commit their bodies to the ground; earth to earth, ashes to ashes, dust to dust; in the sure and certain hope of the Resurrection to eternal life."

A chorus of *amen* rose from the gathered mourners. Rachel watched as her parents' coffins were lowered inch by inch, into the dark pit in front of her. She wondered why they were bothering; it wasn't as if her parents were actually in there. The police had told her that her parents' remains had been 're-moved', as there had been very little left to bury. But it had been insisted in their Will that they have a full ceremony. So, here she was, playing the obedient, loving daughter.

She looked up at the faces standing around the graveside. Becky was standing next to her, resting her hand on Rachel's shoulder. She was glad her friend was there for support. Every now and then, she could feel eyes boring into her skull. She didn't recognise many of the people; a few Aunts and Uncles, some old family friends, but that was it. And even those she did recognise gave her nothing but scornful looks, or avoided all eye contact completely. Nobody wants to associate themselves with a crazy person, she realised, as the coffins landed with a final dull thud. It was just the way she liked it; no awkward moments, or any people offering her pity. She would just get the funeral out of the way and then go as far away from the town as she could. In a way, she was thankful that she would never have to come back to Willows Peak ever again. The place held too many memories of that night.

After the priest had said his final words, the mourners shuffled away. Etiquette decreed that Rachel be the last to leave. She waited with Becky until the final person had left, before wandering over to the priest.

"Thank you Father, it was a beautiful ceremony."

"Your parents will be sorely missed on a Sunday. Such tragic circumstances. Have the police found the cause of the fire?"

"They said no one could have prevented it, just one of those things," Rachel replied, her voice almost catching on the words. "It was faulty wiring that started it."

"My thoughts and prayers are with you, Miss James. Will you be staying in Willows Peak for long? It would be nice to see you in church."

Rachel noticed the raised eyebrows. She smiled. "I don't think so, Father."

The two friends continued walking toward the cars. A gust of wind blew the fallen leaves across the field, creating a patchwork of browns and oranges. Rachel closed her eyes and let the tension in her blow away on the breeze. The silence of the afternoon filled her.

"Are we heading to the wake?" Becky asked, snapping her out of the moment.

"I suppose I should."

"You don't have to if you don't want to. I can go back and -"

"For God's sake, stop fussing over me," Rachel yelled, wrenching her arm free. "I need to do this, they're my parents not yours."

"Okay, there's no need to snap at me. I was only asking."

"Well don't, alright?"

"What the hell is wrong with you? Ever since we got here you've been different."

Rachel walked off. She didn't bother to look back; Becky would follow eventually. She was used to Rachel's off moments by now. It wasn't fair that everybody just assumed she was too frail to cope. Well screw them all, she fumed, they would just have to get over it. She had.

"Rachel, stop, please tell me what's wrong? I'm trying to understand, but I can't."

She spun on her heels. "Oh I don't know, maybe my parents died? Just maybe I didn't get to…" She stopped short, taking a deep breath. "Just forget it, okay. I'll see you at the hotel."

"Aren't you coming in the car?"

"I feel like a walk."

Rachel had begun walking away over the windswept cemetery before she had even finished her sentence. Her arms hugged her tight, as she walked head down, back to the sleepy little town. The rain was beginning to pour now. Her umbrella sprung into action. Everything was so hard being back home. There was so much anger and frustration that she thought she had buried, sprouting to the surface like dead flowers coming back to life. She knew it was out there, looming in the distance. There was just no way to block the thought of it from her mind, not now that she knew it had survived the fire.

"Hey gorgeous, need a ride?"

The familiar voice startled her. She stopped in her tracks not realising that she had already made it to the outskirts of town. She turned to look at the car.

"Hey Rach, you alright?"

"Nathan, what're you doing here?"

"Ummm, I live here. Remember?" Nathan chuckled. His warm, dark brown eyes smiled at her.

"I just thought you would've been long gone by now?"

"Nah," Nathan replied, looking straight ahead. "I'll be here until they build a monument dedicated to me."

Rachel returned the laugh. "Well you're one person I didn't expect to see."

"I could say the same about you." Nathan's eyes softened. "I'm sorry to hear about your folks."

She dropped her eyes to the floor. "So am I."

There was a moment's silence before she spoke. "So, what do you do these days?"

"I pick up young, drenched women off the street." His boyish grin had returned. "I'm a deputy sheriff now."

"Oh wow, followed your Pa's footsteps then?"

"Yeah, it was a natural progression." There was another awkward silence. The rain was pouring now. "So, where're you headin'? I can give you a lift."

"Oh, ummm, it's okay, I could do with the walk."

"Hey, it's a torrent out here. Nobody likes getting wet. Hop in."

Rachel lowered her umbrella and did as she was told. It was just like old times, as the two drove off in to the rain.

***

Sad faces filled the reception room of the bed and breakfast, as the guests reminisced about the past and the tragic circumstances under which Mr and Mrs James lost their lives. *Could've happened to anyone; they'll be missed; it's such a loss.* Rachel did her best to be the perfect host, keeping herself busy by carrying around platters of food and making sure people had coffee, or in some cases, wine. She knew they were talking about her. Gossiping about what happened. Seeing Nathan after her years of self-imposed exile had lifted her spirits a little. He had been very fortunate.

She looked out over the gathering, searching for him. Thin, wispy grey clouds hung over the heads of the smokers like haunting spectres. A shudder crept up her spine, as she remembered the smell from that night. Fire seemed to be a constant in her life. Now it had killed her parents.

"You alright, Rach?" Nathan asked, placing a gentle hand on her shoulder.

"You've gone really pale."

"There you are. I've been looking for you."

"Have you now?" he replied, a slight rising of his eyebrows pulling his face in to a cheeky grin. "What can I do for you, ma'am?"

"Take me away from here," she replied staring at nothing in particular.

"Not enjoying being back in sunny Willows Peak then?"

"I'd rather be anywhere, but here."

"I don't blame you," Nathan replied, taking a sip from his

coffee. "Not after what you went through."

Rachel shifted uncomfortably. "Don't you start."

The two of them stood for a few moments just watching the crowd. Light filtered through the net curtains of the rear windows. Rachel could see Becky talking to Mr and Mrs Phelps in one corner of the room. Every now and then she would look up, giving Rachel a look as if to say, *are you okay?* Each time, Rachel replied with a smile that said, *I'm fine.* But she wasn't. Far from it. She could feel the tension rising in her like a crescendo of a chaotic, classical piece. Every time she tried to force it down, it came back with a vengeance.

"I am sorry you know," Nathan said, breaking through the silence that had built up like a wall between them.

Rachel hadn't even remembered he was there. "Sorry? For what?"

"For not being there that night. If I had, maybe I could've stopped him."

She didn't get a chance to reply. Two of her parents' friends were heading straight for them. They greeted her with open arms. Fake sympathy.

"Oh Rachel dear, you must be simply distraught. Such a tragic loss."

The smell of cigarettes and wine filled Rachel's nostrils, as Mrs Krupp leaned in to plant a kiss on her cheek.

"Your Daddy'll be a big loss down at the golf course," Mr Krupp added, placing himself behind his wife.

"Thank you."

"Have the police found the cause of the fire yet?" Mrs Krupp asked, aiming the question at Nathan.

"The official line is that it was faulty wiring," he looked at Rachel. "But the investigation isn't quite finished yet."

Mrs Krupp took Rachel by the hand. "You poor thing, having to deal with all this on top of everything that happened to you here. Jack and I feel you're so brave coming back."

The tension was rising in her again. "Stop."

"The horrendous time you had," Mrs Krupp continued.

"They never did find the bodies."

"Please stop." Her body was shaking. Becky was trying to force her way through the oblivious mourners.

"Poor kids. Although I never did like that Chelsea."

The words were drilling in to her pounding head.

"I think Rachel's had enough, Mrs Krupp. It's been a long day," Nathan butted in.

But she was in full flow now. "Such a nice boy, who'd have thought he
could -"

"For God's sake, shut up," Rachel screamed. The room stopped dead, as if someone had flicked a switch. "Just shut up. I know the bodies weren't found. Chelsea was my best friend, do you think I'd ever forget what *he* did." She was shrieking now. Mrs Krupp stood there as if she had been shot. "He wasn't a nice boy, he was the devil. He took everything from me. My friends, my home, almost my sanity. Everything. So, I left, hoping to forget. Forget him, forget this hell hole. Instead, I find the house rebuilt and everyone treating me like a freak with a disease." The tears finally broke. "I didn't even get to say goodbye to my parents."

She made a bolt for the stairs. Condemning eyes bored in to her, as she fled the now silent room. She wanted to get out, get away from people. She wanted to hide herself somewhere and disappear.

"Hey, Rach, wait. Come back," Becky called after her.

Rachel just ignored her friend and continued running up the stairs to their room.

***

#Rachel didn't know how long she had been sobbing on the bed; the pillow case was soaked through. The light in the room had dimmed, as the sun made its way around to the back of the building. Nobody had bothered to come up and check to see if she was alright. In a way, she was glad of that.

She sat up. The constant droning of conversation buzzed through the floor from downstairs. In her hand was the last happy memory she had of her parents. Her raw eyes stared hard at the graduation photo. It had been a bright, sun-filled day that had culminated in a huge party. She could remember being filled with giggles, as she had stumbled home with Chelsea at two in the morning, blind drunk. At the time Rachel had hated them for grounding her. But now she could see it was out of love. It was funny, she thought, how old resentments got buried along with the dead. She'd give anything for them to ground her now; take away her credit cards, her car. Anything.

Tears dropped off her cheeks and landed with a faint tap on the shiny surface of the photo. A knock at the door startled her. It was probably Becky come to check on her, she realised.

"Come in," she said, wiping her eyes. The door opened.

"I'm sorry, I was passing and heard crying. Are you alright?"

It was a man poking his head around the door. One she didn't know. Rubbing away the tears, she made herself look more presentable. "I'm fine, thank you."

"No offence, but you don't look it."

Who is this guy? Rachel wondered. "I'm sorry, but do I know you?"

"No I don't think so," the head replied. "I'm pretty new in town."

The man was nothing special, but attractive enough. He had a full head of mousy brown hair sitting on top of a pale, boyish face. "So, what's up?"

Rachel had never been in the habit of telling complete strangers her problems, but something in the man's deep eyes made her want to open up, pour her heart out in an attempt to cleanse the demons inside her. "It's nothing really," she said, putting aside the photo. "I don't even know your name."

"Sorry, the name's David. Doctor David Cochrane."

"Rachel, Rachel James."

"Pleasure to meet you, Rachel."

She had never felt so awkward in her life. Here was this stranger, beaming at her, and she looked an absolute mess.

"You still haven't told me what the tears are for? By the way, you don't know what the shindig downstairs is, do you?"

The tears almost started again. "Yeah," she said, lowering her eyes. "It's my parents' wake."

"Ah, way to go, David. Excuse me, while I remove my foot from my mouth."

David mimed pulling a shoe from his mouth. The laughter it caused scared away any more tears.

"My sympathies," he said, a gentle smile forming on his lips.

"Thank you."

Rachel found herself increasingly attracted to the man standing in the doorway. There was something about him that she couldn't put her finger on. He had an easy manner. Maybe it was because he was a doctor? She mused. It was as if a dark cloud had been lifted. She had almost forgotten there was a wake going on downstairs.

"So, doctor huh?"

"Psychology. I haven't long finished my four year residency. Hence the B&B."

"Ah, I see. Have you been in town long?" she asked, wanting to know more about the stranger.

"No, not really," he replied. "Barely over a month."

"Wow, that long. And you haven't run for the hills?"

David chuckled at her feeble joke. "Nope. I kinda like it. How long have you lived here?"

"This is where I was born." The dark cloud had begun to descend again. "I'm just back in town for a while. Until everything is sorted."

A painful silence entered the room, like a morbid presence. A spectre of the past.

"You'll probably say no, but if you're going to be in town for a while, maybe we could have a chat sometime?" His cheeks had turned a deep red. "Professional of course."

Rachel found his shyness cute. She wanted to say yes. "I think I'm only going to be in town a couple more days."

"That's plenty of time."

She shook her head. "Sorry, I don't think I can."

Out the corner of her eye, she thought she caught a familiar look flash across his face. But as soon as it was there, it was gone. It must've been her imagination, she realised. Maybe it was disappointment?

"Well if you change your mind." David pulled out a business card and placed it on a small table by the door.

"I'm sorry, it's just I'm not much of a talker, so I'd be wasting your time," she replied, trying to sound sympathetic. "Thank you though."

David laughed. "Don't worry about it. I hope everything works out for you."

A slight shuffle behind him drew both their attentions. Becky slotted past and walked in, Nathan not far behind.

"Oh sorry, didn't realise you had company," Becky said with a look of surprise on her face.

"That's okay, I was just leaving." David turned to Rachel with a smile. "Take care."

She felt a pang of regret hit her, as he left the room. She spotted Nathan giving him the evil eye.

"What was he doing here?" Nathan asked.

"Nothing, he was just passing by. He knocked on the door. Any objections?"

"I don't trust him, that's all."

"Wait. Who is he? Why don't you trust him?" Becky asked, her head snapping from side to side, as she looked at each of them in turn.

"His name's David," Rachel replied, before Nathan had a chance to pipe up. "He's a doctor, well, psychiatrist, and he's very sweet." She glared at Nathan.

"If he's a doctor, why is he living here?"

It was a valid question, she thought. "I don't know, maybe he's not found a place of his own." There was a more pressing question ricocheting around her mind. "Why are you so against him?"

"I just am. There's something about him. Call it deputy's instinct."

"Well I like him."

The trio sat in silence. Rachel was beginning to grow tired of the constant awkward tensions that kept growing between her and other people. "I see you two have met." She hoped to change the subject.

"Yeah, Nathan introduced himself after you…" Becky let the sentence trail off. "Anyway, tell me more about this doctor."

"There isn't much to tell," Rachel replied. "He asked if I needed someone to talk to."

"Rachel, I've got to get back on duty," Nathan butted in. "Maybe I'll come back later."

"Oh, okay. It was so good to see you again."

"Yeah, and you," he replied. "Take it easy."

He closed the door behind him, leaving the two girls alone in the room.

"What's up with him?" Becky asked.

"I don't know," Rachel replied, puzzled. It was really unlike him to act like a jerk, she thought, her head racing with so many new emotions. He had always been so sweet and shy when they had been friends in high school. How time changes people, she realised.

A yawn erupted from her. She felt as though she could sleep for a week.

"It's been a long day," Becky remarked.

"Tell me about it."

"There aren't many people left, just a few after more free wine. Shall we get back to them?"

"I suppose I should. I feel like such an idiot."

"Don't worry about it. No one noticed."

Rachel let out a small laugh. "Thank you for all this."

"Don't mention it," Becky replied. She bounced off the bed. "Right, let's get back then."

"Just give me a sec."

"Okay."

Becky pulled the door to, as she left. Rachel took one last look at the memory she held in her hand. That summer would live with her for the rest of her life. She folded the photo and placed it back in her purse, trying as hard as she could to block out the memories.

CHAPTER FOUR

The rain hit the black surface of Rachel's umbrella like rapid artillery fire. Tap, tap, tap. The cloud coverage was so thick, the warm rays of the dawn sun couldn't force their way through. It felt like night rather than day. A cold wind battered against her, whipping around her legs. It made the going hard. She had the feeling as though it was trying to drive her back on purpose, to stop her reaching her destination. Maybe it was? She thought. But it wouldn't work. Lowering her head in to the collar of her thick jacket, she pushed on.

She didn't know how long she'd been walking. Her feet had just led the way; first through the rain soaked streets, then out over the sweeping fields, along the hard shoulder of the highway. Time just seemed to slip past as she walked. It didn't seem to matter how long she had been gone, or how far outside the town she was, she knew her feet would take her somewhere.

Her mind moved forward and backwards between the past and present, trying to weigh up which one was worse. Every now and then, a car would stream past her in a hazy blur, spitting rain water up behind it. But even though her eyes perceived it, she paid no attention. In the back of her mind, she knew where she was heading and screamed at herself to stop, but she just walked, stuck in a dream from which she couldn't escape.

Before long, the road began to incline upwards, the grey sky melding with grey treetops, looming larger with every step. Within the next five minutes, *it* would be there, she thought, as she climbed higher up the hillside. Its pointed roof would stick out above the ridge line, stretching upwards, jagged and dangerous, like a knife jutting into the heavens.

Her steps were slow. Her breathing shallower than it had been before. The constant drumbeat of blood in her ears was like a marching song, edging her ever closer. She lowered her umbrella and grasped at her hands in an attempt to stop them shaking. This is a bad idea, she thought, still moving forwards, never stopping. Her mind screamed at her to turn back, to go into town and forget about this stupid need that had pounced on her during the fluid waking moments of the dawn. There was some glimmer of false hope buried deep down inside her, pushing her on. Maybe she had made a mistake? Maybe it was just a similar looking place? This was a small town; a lot of the buildings looked the same, especially the farmhouses. Over and over again she tried to convince herself that she had been wrong. Nobody would ever want to rebuild that thing. And houses couldn't just rebuild themselves. Could they?

Looking up, she realised she had already reached the top of the hill. The air stuck in her throat like a piece of hard food, as she inhaled sharply.

It was there. The house of wood, renovated to its former glory. Gone was the flaky paint and rotten wood of the porch, replaced by a bright white coat stretching along its walls. The wooden steps leading up to the front door were now perfectly square wooden planks, rather than rough, crooked teeth. The windows were no longer encrusted with years of dirt and grime. It was all a façade. Still they looked out over the countryside like malevolent eyes, dark and dreary, as if they were watching for something, waiting like a coiled cobra for a time when they could strike again. The long shadow cast over her felt frigid and desolate. No amount of cleaning, or decorating, could remove the unwholesome stain that the building had left on the surrounding area. On her own psyche.

This is ridiculous, she thought. The house hadn't done anything to her, it had been *him*. The house itself was just a building, an inanimate object that couldn't do anything except look creepy. So why did she feel such hatred towards it? The dolls, she thought. Nothing could explain the dolls. Anger and bitterness ate away at her. She hated it and everything it represented.

As if on autopilot, she moved forward and around to the right of the house. The bleak silence seemed to permeate everything, seeping in to her pores. The isolation was almost suffocating. It clawed at her mind, trying to find a crevice, any recess in which it could embed itself. There's nothing out here, she thought, as she continued her tour around the fringes of the building. There was just the house. And of course, the blackbirds that plagued the farms in the area. The town had always had an abundance of them. Two were perched on the dark roof, their beady eyes watching her, as she walked along the final wall. One of them had some kind of dead animal carcass hanging from its beak. A mouse, maybe? Whatever it was, it looked like a horrific way to die. She shuddered. The birds were another thing she hated about the place.

Rachel was back at the front now. She had noticed something; no matter where she stood to look at it; front, back, side, it was still the same old building. She supposed it always would be like that. At certain points, it had felt as though it was going to come alive and lurch forward, crushing her beneath its huge mass. In a way, she wished that was possible.

Her hand had started to tremble. Bending over, she picked up a reasonable sized stone. It felt sharp and harsh in her smooth palm. It would do.

She stood up and launched it at the house.

"I hate you, I hate you!"

The rock hit the wall, chipping off some of the new paint, before falling lifeless back to the floor. She selected another.

"You ruined my life," she screamed, hurling the stone.

It struck. Then another, and another. Her breathing had quickened, going in and out with short, ragged bursts.

"You took everything from me."

Deep down, she knew it wasn't the house she was aiming at; the house had done nothing, except act as the setting to her nightmare. But she couldn't stop herself. The person she wanted to get at wasn't here. Her seething anger had broken through to the surface and was in full swing. There was no stopping it.

More and more rocks ricocheted off of the white wooden walls of the building. Scarring them. The final stone flew through the air and struck the window with a loud crash that seemed to reverberate around the hillside.

She stopped, the sound pulling her out of the maelstrom that was her fury. She took a deep breath trying to slow her heart rate. She looked up at the broken window. The jagged hole in the black pane made it look even more sinister. But the whole event had felt like a cleansing, a releasing of the pressure valve that had been slowly rising since she had arrived in town. There was no telling how long it would last. No doubt it would bubble and boil over again before her time was done. She prayed that she would have left town by then.

She turned to leave, stopping only once to look over her shoulder at the house. It was still. The only thing was the ever present silence. She closed her eyes and walked away.

What she missed was the face staring out of the broken window. Smiling.

***

The figure moved away from the window, gliding along the floorboards. A single blackbird sat in the corner, pecking at a rat carcass.

"I know they can't find out."

"If they find out the truth it'll be down to you. Could you forgive yourself if they do?"

"Just leave me alone!" The figure shouted, causing the bird to look up.

It was pitch black in the bedroom. A small shaft of sunlight peeked through a crack in the curtains. Unlike the rest of the house, the upstairs hadn't been touched yet. It was like a blank canvas waiting to be transformed in to a work of art. Something beautiful. But the old furniture that had survived the fire was covered in dirt and dust. Cobwebs adorned the lampshade and every available ceiling corner.

"Well could you forgive yourself if people find out the truth?" A silence passed for a few moments. "Well? You know what your brother did. You'd be ruined."

"NO!" The figure spat, slamming a fist against the wall. A small cloud of dust leapt in to the air.

The figure sat alone in the living room of the old house contemplating what would happen if the time came to come clean. It probably wouldn't come to that. Most people didn't last long around here anyway. Something always scared them off.

"You won't take me like you did the rest."

"I want revenge on that bitch."

"We shall see. Nothing happens to her before I get the full story of what occurred here."

Silence.

The figure moved around the house, doing bits and pieces before leaving out the front door. Rachel was long gone. Call it chance, or fate, but whichever it was, it was a fine thing. She was exactly what was needed. It would be time for answers soon. Everything would work out just fine.

***

It hadn't taken Rachel long to walk back in to town. By the time she had reached the bed and breakfast, the heavy rain had turned in to a light drizzle. Even the sky was beginning to brighten, the sunlight finally fighting its way through the dense grey cloud. She lowered her umbrella and let the damp air hit her face, refreshing her before she went back inside. It was as if she was washing away the previous hour spent travelling to and from the house. It felt good.

She tried not to make a sound, as she entered the small hallway. Off to her left, the dining room was beginning to stir with the first, early morning patrons eating their complimentary breakfast. The smell of bacon and eggs drifted down the hallway straight to her nostrils. She felt like Eve being tempted by the Apple, and her mouth filled with saliva. The tantalising aroma was tempting. She put a hand across her stomach. No, the last thing she needed was people coming and talking to her. The best thing would be to get back up to her room, lock the door and shut out Willows Peak. At least until her meeting with the sheriff. God knows why he wants to see me, she thought, crossing the threshold. With any luck, it'll be to tell me that the investigation is over and that I can go home. That was all she wanted. To go home.

The door made an audible click, and it swung back into its slot. Without skipping a beat, she spun around and threw herself at the first few steps. She knew what was coming. It was inevitable.

"You seem to be in a hurry, dear," Mrs Ryan said, making no attempt to hide the distaste in her voice. "May I offer you some breakfast?"

Rachel turned around to face the annoying little woman. She was standing in the doorway to the parlour, two beady little eyes searching for any hint of gossip.

"No thank you, Mrs Ryan. I think I'll just return to my room."

"Been anywhere interesting?"

"Just out for a stroll."

"At this hour? It's far too early for just a stroll. I hope you aren't thinking of bringing a gentleman back in. I won't have any of *that* going on in my establishment."

Mrs Ryan was beginning to grate on Rachel's last nerve. She could feel that familiar tingling in her hands. The same she had felt at the house. She bit back her tongue.

"No, of course not," she replied, hoping her voice didn't sound strained. "I just needed some fresh air."

"Oh, fresh air, I see. Well remember what I've told you. I know the stories. The first sign of trouble and you're out of here. I don't want my place -"

"Will that be all?" Rachel cut in.

Fire burned hot in her eyes. How dare this evil little woman accuse her of anything? What did she know? Nothing, that's what. She was just another one of the small town gossips vying for her pound of flesh. Well, she wasn't going to get it. Rachel had already noticed her inching backwards.

"Y-yes, that'll be all. You've been warned."

Mrs Ryan shot off in the direction of the dining room, as Rachel bolted up the stairs, her feet pounding on the well-worn wood. She no longer needed to be quiet. The damage had already been done. The tranquil calm she felt outside, gone, along with every ounce of love she had for her hometown. The bitch had been just like the rest; too quick to judge something they didn't understand.

She slammed the bedroom door without thinking. Becky flew upright in the bed, her back so erect, she looked like Frankenstein sitting on the operating table.

"What the hell?" she said, still half asleep.

"Sorry, it's just me. I didn't mean to wake you."

Becky looked at the clock. "Where have you been at this hour?"

"Nowhere," Rachel replied. "Just walking."

"Just walking?"

"Yes."

"And you're alright?"

"Yes, I'm fine. It's nothing a nice, warm soak under the shower can't fix. You just go back to sleep."

Becky threw the cover over her head. By the time Rachel had stripped down to her underwear, she was fast asleep. Soft snores filled the silent void in the room.

CHAPTER FIVE

The noonday sun blazed through the white spectral clouds over the downtown area of Willows Peak. Citizens of the sleepy town ran to and fro between the small shops that made up Main Street. The area was experiencing unusually high temperatures for that time of year. The weather forecasters would later call it an Indian summer. Whatever it was, it wasn't normal.

Rachel sat at the back of the quaint little café at a secluded table. She looked out of place, sitting in front of her laptop, but she had to sit down. And anyway, there was something about the place she liked.

Her feet throbbed under the constraints of her Nike trainers. First there had been some papers for school that needed dropping off at the post office; then she had to rush across town in order to make a 10 o' clock meeting with the sheriff. Usually she was solid and wouldn't care. But today was different. Today she wasn't on her game.

The cursor on the blank Word document blinked at her, as if it was frustrated at not moving across the page. In her left hand she was fiddling with the doctor's business card. Why shouldn't I take him up on his offer? She mused. It had been three years for Christ's sake. He was a professional. What was she afraid of?

Her right hand absently fondled with the silver inscribed locket around her neck.

To my high-school sweetheart: Always and Forever.
Yeah, until….
"Howdy Little Lady."
Nathan's voice made her jump. He stood there beaming

at her.

"Fancy a coffee?"

"If you're buying," Rachel replied with a smile.

She sat for several moments watching him at the counter. He was such a good friend. If the chips were down, then she knew he was a man that could be counted on. But his reaction the other day had taken her by surprise. Her mind, like a child reaching for the cookie jar at the back of the cupboard, just couldn't grasp what it meant. Was he jealous? He had never shown any romantic interest in her. And it wasn't as if David had asked her on a date. It was professional curiosity. Nothing more. So why would he be jealous?

Snippets of conversation filtered through over the Barista's clamouring: the weather, the trouble in the MiddleEast, public scandals, the mundane topics of conversation. To a lot of people they wouldn't have been mundane, but to her they meant nothing. Her mind was too full.

Nathan returned to the table carrying two steaming cups of black liquid.

"Thank you," she said, as he sat down opposite her.

"No problem. How're you feeling?"

"Tired."

"I can imagine," he replied. "Pa mentioned he'd seen you this morning."

Rachel let out a deep sigh. "Yeah, he did. Not that there was much point. Isn't there anything you can do?" She so desperately wanted to go home.

"I'm sorry Rach, my hands are tied. This is a small town. We've only got thirty officers and ten of those are part-time."

"But it's ridiculous." The frustration at getting nowhere was bubbling beneath the surface. "It was either an accident, or not."

"We're not sure," Nathan replied, lowering his eyes to the table.

"For Christ's sake, how can you not be sure?" Rachel shouted at him.

Tentative heads turned in their direction.

"Rach, calm down. We're doing all we can. These things take time."

"I just want to be able to go home. How can they even suggest I'm a suspect, I wasn't even in town."

Nathan looked at her square in the eyes. "It's just routine. We have to investigate every possible avenue, just in case. Nobody really believes you could be involved. Especially not me."

He smiled at her. The warmth and genuine care in his eyes melted away the tension. It wasn't until that moment that Rachel realised how much she had missed him. She smiled back. "Thank you. I'm sorry I was being a bitch."

"That's okay," he replied. "No one can blame you."

Moments ticked by, as the two of them sat in silence. Tiny dust mites danced in the air, as the lazy sunlight burned through the glass window, causing them to flash silver.

Rachel took a short sip of her espresso, rolling the bitter black liquid over her tongue. Not once did she take her eyes away from the window. How long would she have to wait? She wondered. A part of her was pleased to be back in town among old friends and familiar places. Over the road was the shop where she bought her prom dress; next to that was the small cinema, where she had her first date. There had been so many good times. A lot of them with the guy sitting opposite. But there was another part of her. The part that knew this was the last time she would return home.

"Nathan," she said, not looking up from her coffee. "I've missed not having you around. You're about the only thing I *have* missed around here."

"I've missed you too, Slugger. The place hasn't been the same without you. Without any of you."

"Yeah." The silver locket around her neck was cold against her warm skin. Why did she still wear it? She didn't want to think about that now. "When I go home, promise you'll come and visit."

She noticed Nathan's shoulders slump. He took a long sip

of his coffee.

"I'll try," he said, no longer looking at her. "With work and all. You know how it is."

"I won't take no for an answer. I'm sure Becky would like to see you again." She let the insinuation hang in the air. It went unnoticed. "I think she likes you."

"I doubt it, we only just met."

"Well, she hasn't stopped talking about it since the funeral," Rachel replied. "Maybe, you should ask her out on a date?"

"Maybe," Nathan said. He fidgeted in his chair. "Talking of dates, maybe we -"

A loud crash from the back of the shop cut the sentence short. Rachel turned her head away to see what the noise was. It was only a mousy waitress with tomato red cheeks; a result of her clumsiness with the tray. Rachel turned back. As she did so, her face lit up.

"Doctor Cochrane." The words fumbled from her lips before she could stop them.

David looked over his shoulder with a frown. His eyes roamed over the patrons of the café. As soon as they locked onto Rachel, she felt her stomach drop. He smiled at her, picked up his coffee and walked towards her.

"Doctor Cochrane, hi," she said, feeling like a schoolgirl with a crush. Nathan fidgeted again.

David swept back his fringe. "Hello, Miss James. I didn't think I'd have the pleasure of seeing you again. I hope all is well?"

"Things could be better, but on the whole, I'm not too bad."

"Good." He turned to Nathan. "Afternoon, deputy, keeping the streets safe I hope."

"We do our best," Nathan replied at the joke, not bothering to look up.

Rachel could see the tension mounting on his face. The air had become awkward.

"Doctor Cochrane -"

"David, please."

She smiled. "David, would you like to join us?"

"I've got a break now. I'd love to."

David sat down in the seat next to Rachel. If looks could kill, then she would have dropped stone dead on the floor. Nathan was scowling at her.

She gave him a quick kick under the table. "Have you met David before, Nathan?"

"We've met a few times, yeah." He picked up his cup. His eyes glared at her through the steam as he drank. Rachel ignored it.

"The deputy and I met not long after I arrived in town. In fact, he was one of the first people I met."

"Oh really," she replied. "How was that?"

"Wow, is that the time. I really must be going." Nathan jumped out of his chair like a Jack-in-the-Box. "It was a pleasure seeing you again, doctor."

"But, you haven't finished your coffee," Rachel said, bemused. "Stay a bit longer."

"Sorry. Can't. Sheriff Ross'll have my balls if I don't get back. Say hi to Becky for me."

"Okay, bye."

Nathan was gone before the last word had left her lips.

It was the second time he had done that to her in a week and it was starting to worry her. She didn't want things to be awkward between them. Maybe it had been too long? She thought. People change over time.

David cleared his throat, pulling her mind back to him.

"I'm sorry." Her cheeks turned red. "He's normally a really nice guy. I'm not sure what's got into him."

"Please, don't worry about it. The deputy has a very stressful job, keeping the town safe and all."

Rachel smiled. He was so understanding. The more time she spent with him, the more relaxed she became. It was the first time in her life that she felt as though she could open up to someone. Tell him anything and not be judged.

He motioned to her empty cup. "More coffee?"

"Please."

He left her sitting there, while he strolled over to the counter. The café was heaving now. She fondled the business card under the table, at the same time biting her lip. She didn't know what to do. This guy was a professional psychiatrist, but she had seen those before. They hadn't helped, only made things worse. Maybe David was different? Maybe she had finally met someone that could pluck her out of the past?

David returned with the coffee. "I wasn't sure if you took sugar."

"No, it's fine. Thank you."

"You're welcome."

The two of them sat there drinking coffee, time flying past. Rachel felt as though she was in a different world. All her cares and worries felt as though they were from another life; someone else's life that she had read about in a horror novel. She was becoming increasingly intrigued by the man sitting next to her. He was charming, polite and funny. They chatted about everything from the weather to the result of the local High School football game. He didn't know her. There were no connections to her past with him. She was lost in the velvet softness of his voice.

"… and that's how I met Nathan."

The end of his sentence made her ears prick up. "I'm sorry, how did you meet?"

There was concern in his face. "Are you alright? You look pale."

"Yeah, I'm fine." The dark cloud was beginning to descend on her again. "I just zoned out for a second."

"Does that happen often?" David asked.

Only since I've been back. "No, not at all."

There was silence. If she was going to ask, now was the perfect time. She sipped at her coffee. "Doctor -"

"David."

"If it's still okay," she asked, her fingers furiously fiddling with the business card. "Could I take you up on that offer of a chat?" Her face turned a deep scarlet. "Whenever you're free."

"Of course. If you come down to the office, my secretary will -"

"I was hoping we could make it..." She paused to think of the right words. "Less formal."

"Ah, I see," David replied. He shifted in his seat and took a large gulp of his coffee.

Rachel had to think quick. "I know it's not professional for you. It's just, I've tried the formal thing. It didn't work. I closed off completely. Maybe chatting over a dinner table would help me to open up?" Well done Rachel, she thought. That's the way to be subtle.

He grinned. "I'm sure that'll be fine. I hear Costello's over on Lonergran is very nice. Would that be okay?"

She could feel her heart racing. "That would be lovely."

"I finish my shift tonight at the hospital around eight. I could stop by your room at nine?"

Was this moving too fast? She wondered. She'd hoped for a couple more days. Butterflies were going crazy in her stomach. His steel blue eyes fixed right on her. If she didn't take the chance now, she never would. "That'll be great."

"Good. Nine it is then."

They sat there for another half an hour, finishing their coffees. David looked at his watch. "Well, I best be getting back. I'll see you tonight at nine o'clock."

"Okay."

"Bye."

As the door of the cafe closed behind him, Rachel slumped in her chair. Relieved. She had no idea what had come over her. She would never have asked out a guy she didn't know before. Now she was nervous.

She looked out of the window. The sunshine had hidden behind some clouds. The air felt stormy. She peered across the street. A single blackbird was perched on top of the box office at the cinema. She rubbed at her eyes. Was it looking at her? Don't be silly, she thought, it's just the nerves.

She shut down her laptop, packed it away and gulped the last dregs of her coffee. When she turned to pick up her bag, she noticed the bird had gone.

CHAPTER SIX

Nathan had been driving around town aimlessly in the car for two hours since leaving the café. As usual the town was quiet; dispatch hadn't sent out any emergency calls all day. Under any other circumstances, it would have been a blessing. But not today. The last thing he needed was time to think. His mind had been spinning like the wheels beneath him, bringing him back to the same conclusion over and over. It was happening again. For the second time in his life, Rachel was choosing somebody else over him. How could it be? He thought. Was he that unlucky? Of all the people in the town she could have chosen, she had to choose him. David was bad news. Deep down inside him Nathan knew it. He just couldn't work out why. Well, he was damn sure he was going to find out.

The traffic lights above him turned red. The squad car ground to a halt. He licked the sweat off of his top lip, trying to keep his eyes fixed on the road. He knew it was there; the place that had caused all his recent problems. There was that familiar gnawing sensation at the back of his brain. It wouldn't hurt to go in for one, he thought, resisting the urge to turn his head in the direction of his nemesis. He knew if he saw it, the day would be over. He would sink himself into that black pit, which was getting harder and harder to climb out of. And there wasn't time for that. If he was going to stop the past repeating itself, then he had to stay on track. His own peace of mind depended on it.

The light turned green and Nathan set off, letting out a small sigh of relief. He had managed to resist it, but promised the demon inside him that he would return later. At an appropriate time. If there ever was such a thing.

He spent the next thirty minutes parked outside the café. He needed answers, but didn't know where to look for them. If only he could find something, a bit of dirt, something to pin on the doctor, then he could show it to Rachel and she would know the truth. He owed it to her. If he hadn't let her go the last time a new guy came into her life. If he had been more forceful, instead of walking away. Life may have turned out different. All he had ever wanted was for her to look at him the way he looked at her. He had to find something. But where?

The squad car revved into life, as Nathan turned the key. A thought had struck him. He had no idea where it came from. But it was better than nothing. He reached over and picked up the radio microphone.

"Dispatch, this is Deputy Ross, do you copy?"

This is dispatch.

"Hey Connie, I need you to do me a favour. Can you look up any files on the Langrishe case? It'll be in the archive."

Nate, I don't have access.

"Like that's ever stopped you before. Please Connie. I'll buy you dinner."

Always the charmer. I'll see what I can do.

"Thanks Connie, I owe you. I need you to look up family records, see if there's any connection to a Doctor David Cochrane. I'm also going to need to know who owns the old farm house. You know the one, just outside town."

Why do you need to know all that?

"Just a hunch."

Okay, I'll see what I can do.

"Oh, one other thing. Let's just keep this between me and you for now. It'd be best if the Sheriff didn't know anything about it."

If you say so.

"You're a star. Talk to you later."

Nathan put the microphone back on its hook. If he wanted answers, then where better to start than the beginning.

***

It didn't take him long to reach his destination. The house stood tall in front of him, as he stepped out of the squad car. He had never liked the place. There was something about it; an oppressive feeling that filled him with dread. He imagined it was similar to the feeling of staring down a predator. An involuntary spasm crept down his spine. At least it wasn't as bad as it used to be. Somebody was making a real effort to return the building to its former glory.

He had no idea why he had come. It was as if the idea had popped out of nowhere, smashing through his skull like a sledge hammer. As far as he knew, David had no connection to the place. When the shit hit the fan three years ago, David had probably never even heard of Willows Peak, let alone having anything to do with the house. But there was something. An air of mystery to the guy that Nathan just couldn't let go of. He had swept in to town and convinced everyone that he was this mild mannered psychiatrist trying to help the poor folk. Well I'm not fooled, Nathan thought. Like the house being all bright and shiny, it was all fake.

A crowing blackbird caught his attention, as it swooped overhead and landed on the porch roof. Its black eyes looked right through him. The answers were here. He knew it. It was just a case of finding them.

He walked up the wooden steps towards the front door, surprised to see there wasn't any workmen around. By all accounts, Jonathon Kane and his boys had been up here, every day for the past two weeks doing the place up. So somebody definitely owned it. If he could get inside, then maybe he could find out who. But there was no way a judge would grant a search warrant without due cause. And there was no doubt in his mind that he would be lucky enough for the door to be unlocked.

Reaching out, he turned the cold knob. It was shut firm. He quickly looked over his shoulder and took out his pick lock. There was nobody around. Within a few minutes the door was gaping wide open. He took one more look around, then stepped over the threshold.

The smell of fresh paint hit him full in the face. The workmen obviously hadn't left that long ago. They were no doubt on a lunch break. Nathan realised he would have to be quick in case they came back from wherever they had gone.

The workmen were doing a good job on the place. The old dank and dreary décor had been replaced with pastel paints and brand new furniture. There was no mistaking it for what it was; a country farmhouse. But now it had a hint of modernisation. He could still see that it wasn't quite finished. The new gas pipes running through the living room hadn't been boxed in yet and the table surfaces were still covered with dust sheets to avoid paint drips ruining them. Apart from that, it was all but finished.

He didn't want to waste too much time admiring the decorating. He quickly got himself together and started searching the house. First he swept through the living room and then the adjacent kitchen diner. He had no idea what he was looking for. If he could find any shred of evidence to connect David to the house, then he would have him, hook, line and sinker. All it would take was a picture, any kind of documentation. But there was nothing downstairs. Whoever owned the place hadn't moved any of their personal belongings in yet.

Nathan decided it might be upstairs. He was about to take a look, when the sound of crunching gravel made his ears prick up. Shit, he thought. The workmen must be back. There was no way he could get out of the house undetected; they would have already seen his squad car, sitting there in the driveway. Why had he been dumb enough to park in front of the house? He fumed. Why had he bothered to come up here in the first place? He'd been clutching at straws. David had absolutely no connection to the house whatsoever. It was stupid to have hoped otherwise.

He ran back to the front door and closed it behind him, hoping that he looked natural. The workmen might have done him a favour.

"Hey there deputy, can I help you?" Jonathon called over,

as he jumped out of his pick-up.

"Hi Mr Kane. I was just checking up on the place. We had a call about an hour ago, saying there was some trouble up here."

"Oh, what kind of trouble? I was in town, picking up some supplies. How did you get in? I made sure the front door was locked when I left."

Nathan looked around, as casually as he could. He spotted the broken upstairs window. "It was a call about some kids throwing stones and damaging the property. They must've broken in because the door was unlocked. I was just checking to see if there had been any damage inside."

"And?"

"It's fine, there doesn't seem to be anything amiss."

Jonathon scratched his chin. "I wonder who made the call. It wasn't any of my boys, they're off today. I'm just up here doing a few bits and pieces. It's not like anybody else would have been walking past. You know what people round here are like, they avoid this place like the plague."

"I know what you mean," Nathan replied. "After everything that's happened, you wouldn't think somebody would want to rebuild the place, let alone live in it."

"Damn straight. It gives me the creeps just having to work here."

This was it. His chance to find answers.

"Just out of interest Jonathon, who *does* own this place now?"

"Damned if I know."

"So you don't know who you're working for?"

"Nope. Everything's being done through a law firm representing the owner. It's all very mysterious if you ask me."

Damn it, Nathan thought. Why wasn't anything going right for him? The house was probably owned by some businessman who wanted to do it up and sell it on for a profit. David probably couldn't even afford a place like this. It had all been for nothing. He was going to lose Rachel again. Maybe she was better off that way?

"Okay, well, let me know if there's any more trouble. It's no doubt just kids pulling some dumb prank. I best get back in to town."

"It's good to see you, Nathan. Thanks for coming to check it out. They'd have my hide, if the place got damaged."

"No problem. Take it easy."

Nathan got back in to his squad car. A flash of anger caused him to lash out at the steering wheel before speeding off back in the direction of the town. The gnawing at the back of his brain had intensified. Screw it, he thought. Time to pay Gloria a visit.

***

Nathan left the squad car in the street adjacent to Logan's Bar, hoping that nobody would realise it was his. He knew people talked about him and his problem, but the less he gave them to gossip about the better.

His hands were shaking as he walked in to the stuffy bar and ordered himself a whiskey.

"Hittin' the hard stuff early today aren't we, Nate?" Gloria asked, pouring the brown liquid.

"Rough day."

"Well honey, you ain't gonna make it any better, burying your face in a glass."

"Thanks for the advice," Nathan replied, taking his drink and moving over to a secluded table in the corner.

As he sat down, the cell phone in his pocket began to vibrate. Reaching in to his pocket and pulling it out, he took one look at the caller I.D. and switched it off. He didn't want to be disturbed. All he wanted was to be left alone this afternoon, so that he could give in to the temptation. It was best that people stayed out of his way.

After the first couple of drinks, he felt fine. He could feel his mood beginning to pick up after the fourth. The time slipped past him quicker than his inhibitions, his sense of right and wrong. People came and went. Nobody bothered him, which he was glad of. He managed to keep them away with a permanent scowl fixed on his face. After the sixth, he promised himself he would only have one more and then get back to the office. Maybe Connie had dug up some dirt? She better have, he thought.

He hated Doctor Cochrane with an intense passion that he hadn't realised he was capable of feeling. The reason Nathan's life had taken a turn straight into a whiskey bottle was his fault. The guy was nothing but a quack, with crackpot theories and an Ivy League diploma. It was his fault that Sheriff Ross was on Nathan's back all of the time. It was his fault Rachel was turning away from him again. Everything was his fault.

The gun on Nathan's hip suddenly felt heavy. It'd be so easy, he thought, draining the last dregs of the whiskey bottle. He was a good cop, it wouldn't be hard to hide the body. His hands shook. No, he thought, he couldn't think like that. At the end of the day, the Doctor hadn't done anything directly to him. When he filed his report, he had only been doing his job. Just like me, Nathan realised. It hadn't been Doctor Cochrane that had ruined his life. It had been his own weakness the day of the shootout that had led him on a downward spiral. He had no one else to blame but himself.

Nathan wandered back over to the bar to get another bottle. The entire room spun as he staggered forward.

"Nother bottle, Gloria."

"I think you've had enough, don't you?"

"You can never have enough."

"If you say so, honey."

She left to get a bottle from the cellar. They didn't keep Nathan's favourite brand behind the bar. He stood there and waited for her to return. He felt a hand on his shoulder.

"Hey Mr Ross, you might want to get out to your car," the bus boy said, looking sheepish.

"And why would that be?"

"I was just passing and could hear the radio going crazy. Whoever was on the other end sounded really pissed with you."

Shit, he thought. "When Gloria comes back up, bring the

bottle out to me."

"Sure, no problem."

Nathan staggered out of the bar as quickly as he could, his legs feeling like jelly. The cold air did little to sober him up on the walk back to the squad car. He got in and tried to compose himself before talking over the radio.

"Dispatch, this is Deputy Ross, go ahead."

Nathan, where the hell have you been? I've been trying to get hold of you for hours.

"Sorry Connie, I was occupied."

There was silence for a few seconds that said more than words ever could. He suddenly felt very ashamed of himself.

"Have you managed to find anything?"

Oh yeah, don't worry, I risked my job for you and found some stuff out.

His heart almost leapt out of his mouth. "What have you found?"

I'm not sure I should tell you.

"Look Connie, I really am sorry, but I need to know that information. I promise I'll make it up to you."

Hmm, well okay. I couldn't find any connection between Doctor Cochrane and the Langrishe family, but I do know who owns the house.

"Who?" Nathan almost shouted it down the line, growing more and more anxious to know.

The same Doctor Cochrane.

That's it, he thought. It wasn't much to go on, but it might be enough to put Rachel off. "Thanks Connie."

No problem.

He put the microphone back on its hook, just as the bus boy bought his bottle of whiskey out to him. Nathan took it. He wanted to go and tell Rachel what he knew straight away. But he doubted whether she would believe him. Not only that, but he didn't think it would be a good idea to drive across town in his condition.

The bottle of whiskey sat on the dashboard, wrapped in

a brown paper bag. He licked his top lip. The hatred for David bubbled inside him. I'll get you, he thought. I'll ruin your life just like you ruined mine.

CHAPTER SEVEN

Nathan had been sitting around the corner in his squad car for ages. Waiting. His anger boiling like milk in a saucepan. Jumped up little prick, he thought. Who does he think he is? He wouldn't let anything happen. Not to Rachel. Not again.

He took a swig from the whiskey bottle in his hand. All he had been able to think about for the last few days was Rachel. He would do anything for her. He loved her. Ever since that first day at elementary school, when he had tripped over her in the sand pit, she'd held his heart. It almost killed him when he heard she was dating Justin back in High School. He was damned if he was going to lose out again.

A streak of lightning illuminated the interior of the car. A shotgun sat in the back seat. His hands shook. A clap of thunder startled him. This was a bad idea. Deep down, he knew it. But he couldn't let her get hurt.

Just then, David Cochrane came walking round the corner. He always parked his car here. He opened the car door and jumped out in one fluid motion. The rain was pouring. He lifted his jacket collar up around his neck. The doctor had spotted him.

"Evening, Nathan. I don't envy you being stuck out in this lousy weather," David shouted over the pattering of the rain on his rooftop. "God knows where this came from!"

Nathan didn't stop. He shoved the other man up against the car.

"Hey, what do you think you're doing?" He pushed Nathan back.

"Stay away from her, you hear me, stay away."

"What? I don't know what you're talking about. Let's go

inside."

Nathan could feel his body shaking. His hands clenched in tandem with his jaw. "Rachel's been hurt enough. I won't let that happen again."

The rain was pelting against them. They stood like two alpha males fighting over a scrap of meat. Nobody else is around, Nathan realised. He could get rid of this problem right now if he chose to. He blinked his eyes.

"Deputy, are you drunk?"

He ignored the question. "I know your secret. Don't care if you know mine. I never liked you. If it hadn't been for Pa forcing me, I never would've put up with your condescending looks and textbook diagnosis. I didn't need you. And neither does Rachel."

He swung a wild fist in an arc towards David's head. It missed by miles, as he stumbled, but managed to stay on his feet.

David bore down on him, causing him to fall in a puddle. "Nathan, you stupid idiot. What the hell do you think you're doing?" He took a deep breath and let it out slowly. He was soaked through. "You're drunk. Go home." He turned back to his car.

Nathan dragged himself up. "You won't hurt her." The image of the shotgun on the back seat of his squad car flew straight to the forefront of his mind. No, he thought. He was drunk. But not that drunk.

"Go home, Nathan," David shouted over his shoulder, as he got into his car.

Deputy Sheriff Nathan Ross stood in the middle of the road, as the doctor drove off. It was hard to tell whether the moisture on his cheeks was pelting rain, or tears. He had failed again. He only hoped this time the consequences wouldn't be as dire as before.

***

"Rach, do you really think you should be going?"

It was the fifth time Becky had asked her that question in

the last hour. It was beginning to grate on Rachel's nerves. She wasn't going to explain again.

Clothes were strewn all over the tiny room. She hadn't expected to be in town this long, so hadn't packed the appropriate date wear. Not that she was going on a date, she reminded herself. Her stomach did another flip.

"You don't even know the guy."

Rachel turned away from the mirror to look at her friend sitting cross-legged on the bed, hugging a floral pillow. It was nice that she cared, but Rachel needed to do this. "I'll be fine."

"I'm sure he's a really nice guy. I just think it's unprofessional to be going on a date."

"It's not a date."

"Then why are you getting all dressed up?" Becky asked, raising an eyebrow.

It was a good question. Rachel had no idea why she was going through all this for a casual dinner. Date?

"Okay, so maybe it is. Is that a bad thing?"

"I don't know. You tell me."

For the first time since lunch, she felt that same oppressive cloud sweep over her. A flash of lightning filtered through the closed curtains. She could feel something wasn't right. She turned back to the mirror. It was just nerves, she thought, taking a deep breath to calm herself. She stared hard at her image in the cracked surface. It would probably be best if she walked down the corridor and told David it was a bad idea. He would understand.

She slammed her fists down hard on the dresser.

Becky jumped. "What the hell?"

"I'm sorry, it's just…" She didn't know what to say. A clap of thunder filled the empty void left by her silence. "I need to do this."

"Okay," Becky replied with a gentle smile. "If you're going to do this, then that top is all wrong."

***

It took another forty-five minutes for Rachel to finish getting ready. The two girls had turned it into quite a jovial event, laughing and joking. It had lifted her spirits. Her stomach still churned and her palms were becoming damper with every passing minute. But she was smiling.

"How do I look?" she asked, giving a twirl.

"You look awesome," Becky replied with an approving look. "Still sure you want to do this?"

"I'm sure."

Rachel sat down in the chair, her eyes checking the clock every thirty seconds.

A watched pot never boils.

What an odd phrase to pop in to her head, she thought. She'd heard someone say it once, but couldn't remember who. She pushed it from her thoughts. The clock said it was nine.

"What're you doing tonight, Becca-Boo?"

"I don't know," Becky replied. "I'll probably stay here."

"You could go down to Logan's Bar. It's pretty cool in there."

"But I'd be alone." She let out a sigh. "I'm better off here."

"I tell you what." Rachel hopped out the chair and went over to a pad on the bedside table. A couple of seconds later she handed Becky a piece of paper with a phone number on it.

Two minutes past nine.

"Ring that number," she said, returning to her chair.

"What is it?" Becky asked.

"It's Nathan's phone number. Ask him out."

"I can't, we just met. Besides, I don't think he's interested in me."

"I think you should give it a shot," Rachel countered. She looked around the boring room. There wasn't even a T.V. "It beats sitting around here all night."

Five past nine.

"You really think I should?"

"Go for it."

Becky pulled out her cell phone and dialled the numbers. Rachel waited in silence. Nothing was happening.

"He's not answering."

"Keep trying," Rachel urged.

"But, what if he's -" She stopped. "Hello, is that Nathan Ross? It's Becky."

Rachel took herself off to the bathroom to give her friend some privacy. She felt good. If she could set those two up, then maybe Nathan would get back to his old self; the sweet, fun loving guy she had known in High School.

She glanced at her watch. It was ten past nine. Where the hell was David? She wondered. She was certain he said he'd be by at nine. He was only down the corridor. Should she wander down the hall and see? What if he was stuck at work? He didn't have her number, she realised. He would have no way of letting her know if he was going to be late.

Becky bounded in to the room, grabbing Rachel's arms. "Nathan said yes, Nathan said yes, Nathan said yes."

Rachel laughed at her friend's antics. It was good to be laughing. "That's awesome, honey. Are you going to Logan's?"

"We sure are," Becky replied, excitement sprawled all over her face. Her eyes suddenly opened wide. "Hey, maybe you and David could join us later? Make it a foursome?"

"That's if he ever turns up." Another two minutes had flown by. Something was amiss, she could feel it. "I'm going to go down to David's room. He should be here by now."

"Want me to come with you?"

"Nah, it's okay. You stay here and get ready. If I find him, I'll pop back in before we leave."

"Alright."

Rachel took one last look at her watch. It was a quarter past nine. The storm was getting worse. Deep down, she silently prayed nothing was wrong.

***

The upstairs corridor of the bed and breakfast was long and dark. It went into a 'T' junction at either end; one way led to more rooms, the other, stairs and a storage cupboard. The décor was much the same as the ground floor. Old. The difference was that it didn't have the same welcoming charm. It was more like a narrow tunnel screaming for people to turn back. Rachel, on the other hand, couldn't. Not if she wanted answers.

She made her way down the narrow passage, heading towards the end with more rooms. All she knew was David's room was to the right. With any luck, she thought, he would be out of his room before she got there.

Dreary faces peered out of ominous grey portraits as she passed by. There was something about black and white pictures that had always unnerved her. She guessed it was because the people in them were usually dead. Ghosts. She shuddered at the thought. They seemed to be even more creepy in the muted, sulphurous yellow light of the hall.

She continued, one step at a time, down the long passage. She could hear the wind howling outside, as it rushed through the old cracks of the building. The sound reminded her of laughter. Maniacal laughter. The kind she had heard before.

There it was again. The image of a whitewashed wooden house in her mind's eye. Her heart rate quickened. Blood pounded in her ears. A picture of Jesus on the crucifix glared at her with his condemning eyes.

You'll burn, bitch!

The lights flickered. Howling. Laughter.

You'll burn in hell!

Rachel's breathing was coming in rapid bursts. The eyes. Oh my God, those eyes.

She groped her way along the cold wall, as she tried to turn back. Disorientated. Tiny beads of sweat had formed on her forehead. The corridor had started to spin. Her voice was stunted. She couldn't call out. There was a face. *His* face.

"Rachel, are you alright?"

She screamed before the darkness took her. The last thing she saw was David catching her in his arms.

Then nothing.

CHAPTER EIGHT

Complete absence of light. The void. Gasping for air. Old faces stare back from the darkness. Submersion. Minutes pass. A watched pot never boils. Chelsea. Dark ominous windows. Heat. The family portrait. Fire all around. No, I don't love you. The swing. Lots of birds. Seconds. Blackbirds. Those eyes like cold steel. Burn in hell, bitch. The dolls. Tim. Blood. So much blood. Justin. Stop.

***

"Rach, oh my God, Rachel wake up."

"Rachel, can you hear me?" It was David's voice. "I think she's coming round. Can you hear me, Rachel?"

Rachel gave several rapid blinks, her mind still not fixed on the present. She was dimly aware of Becky and David hovering over her at the side of the bed. Her head was pounding. She felt as though the local marching band was playing its first gig in there.

She opened her eyes. "Wh-what happened? I was just in the hallway, looking for David."

"I'm here," David replied. "It seems to me as though you fainted. Do you remember anything?"

"No, not really," Rachel replied. "All I can remember is walking down the hallway. I must've had a dizzy spell."

"Can you sit?" Becky asked, her face full of anxiety.

She sat up on the bed. Her eyes hadn't quite focused properly yet, but she could feel herself slowly coming back to normal. The storm outside seemed to have subsided.

"The colour seems to be coming back to your cheeks."

"Thank God," Becky exclaimed. "Do you feel better?"

"Much…" She still felt woozy. "Thank you."

"I think maybe we should give dinner a miss tonight," David said. "It's probably best you stay in bed and rest."

"I'm fine. I just need a few minutes to tidy myself up."

"I don't think that's a good idea, Rach. You should listen to David, he's a doctor."

Rachel turned to look at him. She still couldn't work out what it was that was drawing her ever closer to him. Like a moth to a flame. His face was grave. It had a familiar look even though she had never met him before. "I'll be fine." She looked at her watch. "If we hurry we can still make the reservation."

"Rachy-Bear -"

"Becky, I'm all right. Please, stop fussing over me." She took her friend's hand in hers. "Besides, you have your date to think about."

"I know that look," Becky replied with a grin. "But only if you're positive?"

"I am."

"In that case doc, she's all yours."

"This is against my better judgement, but…" He took one look at Rachel, her eyes bursting with hope. "I'll wait for you downstairs."

David left the room, closing the white door behind him. Rachel moved with caution, as she got out of bed feeling strange. It was a mixture of relief and anxiety. Her image looked back at her from the cracked mirror. She was at a crossroads. She could feel it. If she got everything off of her chest tonight, everything that had built up over the last three years, then she would be cleansed. Her demons would be gone and it wouldn't matter if the house was still out there, or not.

"Are you sure you want to do this?"

"Positive."

She said goodbye to Becky and left, telling her to not wait up.

The corridor seemed less oppressive, but Rachel still didn't feel like hanging around. She fixed her eyes forward and made her way down the stairs, as quickly as she could without showing any outward signs of fear. Her feet slowed at the bottom. Mrs Ryan was standing there, her brow furrowed in to a deep scowl.

"I hope you're not planning to return late tonight. The door will be locked at eleven."

"I wouldn't dream of it, Mrs Ryan," Rachel replied, walking straight past.

The old lady grabbed her by the wrist.

"I warned you," she spat. "I'm not having any of your trouble disturbing the other guests."

Rachel snatched her arm back and rubbed at the finger marks around her wrists. Her eyes were cold with hatred, as she stared hard at the woman.

"Look, you spiteful old bitch, I don't know what I've ever done to deserve your scorn, but I've had enough. You have no idea what happened to me, or my friends, only what the damn gossips have told you." She leant forward to within an inch of the trembling woman's face. "Now back off!"

Feeling satisfied, she spun on her heels and walked out, leaving Mrs Ryan standing there, one hand holding the banister. Her other hand was clutching at a cross around her neck.

***

Rachel was glad the storm had subsided. She hated night driving at the best of times, let alone in the rain. It was still spitting a light drizzle; the kind that was more refreshing than a hindrance. Especially after the high temperature. Grey clouds still hung in the air, sliding across the sky. The soft sounds of Lynyrd Skynyrd playing *Freebird* drifted lazily out of the stereo speakers. She found herself dropping off to sleep.

"Are you sure you're okay?" David asked, never removing his eyes from the road. "It's not too late to turn back."

"Honestly, I'm fine."

She forced herself to stare out of the window in order to stay awake, as the black Toyota Camry cruised down Main Street. More familiar sights streamed past her vision, just like the night she and Becky arrived in town. Fred's Milkshake Bar, where they used to hang out as teenagers, sipping on thick chocolate shakes, or root beer floats; the Fifties style diner, where she had her tenth birthday; Annette's Boudoir. Her prom dress came from there. All the memories flooded her mind. It was as if she had stepped back in time. The time before everything changed.

An unfamiliar sensation came over her. Deep down, she missed this place. The sleepy little town of Willows Peak was her home. She had grown up here. She belonged here.

Just before they broke through the outskirts of town, David turned into the car park adjacent to Costello's Authentic Italian Bistro. He brought the car to a halt.

"Well, here we are. Have you eaten here before?"

"No, I haven't," Rachel replied, looking around at the squat brick building. "I don't think it was here when I left."

"Shall we go in?"

"Let's."

The two of them got out of the car, a small beep announced it was locked. The chilled drops of rain washed away Rachel's sleepiness, as she walked towards the entrance of the restaurant. David offered her his arm and she gladly took it. He's such a gentleman, she realised, a small smile pulling back the corners of her lips. He had even offered to give Becky a lift, but she insisted on getting a cab. Rachel hoped that her friend had found Logan's and not got lost. The thought of her out on the streets late at night was worrying. Especially in this town. No, she thought. Becky would be fine.

As they walked through the entrance, she took a deep breath and let it out slowly. This was it, she thought. There was no going back now.

The interior of the restaurant had a rustic Italian feel to it, with lots of wooden beams and stonework around the walls. Deep green velvet cushions covered the chairs. Across the back of the wall was a perfectly polished bar; the barman was rushing from one end to the other, intent on keeping up with the drink orders. Next to that was the open kitchen dominated by its huge clay oven; the chef hollering instructions to the other kitchen staff. Candle flames swayed in the subdued atmosphere like a hypnotist's pendant. A rotund maître d' greeted them, looking down his nose.

"Good evening, may I help you?"

"Yes, table for two," David replied. "Under the name of Cochrane."

Rachel watched, as the dumpy little man took his time looking through his reservation book. She hated snobbery with a passion.

"Ah yes, this way please."

The maître d' led them to a secluded table at one of the windows looking out over the car park. Perfect for a quiet chat, she realised, butterflies swarming in her stomach again. It was never easy to face the past.

"A waitress will be along shortly to take your orders. Can I get you any drinks whilst you wait?"

"A bottle of red wine would be fantastic," David answered for the both of them.

And with that the maître d' was gone, leaving the two of them alone to look over the dinner menu. Rachel had started chewing her bottom lip.

"Nervous?" David asked.

She looked up at him. "Pardon?"

"You were chewing your bottom lip. I wondered if you were nervous?"

"Oh." It was all she could think of to say. Her cheeks had turned the colour of beetroot. "Maybe a little."

"Please don't be," he replied, adding his usual clean white smile. "I don't bite."

Rachel wondered if he used the same smile on his patients. She smiled back. "I'll try not to."

A tall, wispy haired waitress returned with their wine. She poured each of them a glass, before taking out her crisp white pad. "Are you ready to order?"

David ordered first and then Rachel followed. The waitress dashed off in the direction of the kitchen.

"So, you mentioned a chat?" He looked at her over the soft flame of the candle. His voice calm. Seductive. His eyes penetrating her. They were intoxicating. "Tell me why you left town?"

Rachel was taken by surprise at the suddenness of the question. Why start there? She wondered. "I-I-I'd rather not start with me," she stammered. "Why don't you tell me more about you?"

"Okay." He adjusted himself in the chair. "I had a relatively normal upbringing. Only one other sibling. A younger brother. He died when I was away at college."

"I'm sorry to hear that." Without thinking, she put out her hand and placed it on top of his. She was so drawn in by him, hanging on every word.

"Thank you," he said, not moving his hand away. He cleared his throat. "I graduated from college and decided I wanted to be a clinical psychologist. This is my first job. That's about it really. Over to you."

"There must be more than that?" She wanted to know it all.

David shook his head. "Besides, we're here to talk about you." The smile was back. "Why don't you start at the beginning of the story, as to why you wanted to have this chat?"

Rachel knew she couldn't postpone the inevitable any longer. Her hands shook. The moment to exorcise her Demons had come.

"It's a long story."

"We've got plenty of time."

Outside the rain had started to fall heavily again.

"It was coming towards the end of summer. Everything was beginning to wind down. All the senior class of Willows Peak High School had graduated; bar the odd few drop outs, but nobody really cares about them..."

CHAPTER NINE

    I'd just turned eighteen. It was an amazing feeling to be finally considered an adult. Not that my parents were strict, or anything. Far from it. But being seen as an adult in the eyes of the law gave me a strong sense of freedom; I felt like I could do anything I wanted without consequence. We all did.

    I remember it was a boiling hot day. The sun beat down on my bare shoulders, as Chelsea and I weaved in and out of the shops just off of Main Street. Chelsea was doing her usual 'shop 'till you drop' thing. I just followed.

    "Where'd you wanna go now, Rach?" Chelsea asked, not stopping. The multitude of plastic bags swung like a pendulum on her arm.

    "I don't know," I replied. My feet were killing me. "How about we go get a drink?"

    "Don't be a drag. Daddy upped my credit limit." There was a twinkle in her eye. "Victoria's Secret has just opened up around the corner."

    "Chelsea, we've been walking for ages. I need a rest."

    "But I'm seeing Tim tonight and I want to get something nice." She winked. "To take off."

    "You're such a slut," I said, with a smile. I wasn't getting on her case; she was my best friend. We did everything together. "This is the last shop though."

    "Deal."

    Chelsea sped off in the direction of the lingerie store, me limping behind her like a lost puppy. We had a strange relationship. At times I was both jealous and in awe of her. Who wouldn't be? She had everything a girl could want. Money: her parents were filthy rich. Still are now. And nothing was too much for their little princess. The looks; her hazel eyes matched her mahogany red hair perfectly. It gave her a starlet kind of quality. Of course that meant she was used to guys fawning all over her. She just drifted through life like dust on the breeze, taking everything it threw at her in one simple stride. What did I have? Parents that didn't seem to care less what I got up to, and average looks. I loved her all the same though.

The shop wasn't very big, but it was crammed with eager shoppers. The two of us darted around the place as if our butts were on fire, gathering up skimpy bits of material to try on in the changing rooms. Bargain hunting, Chelsea called it.

"What do you think of this?" she shouted over the rack of bras. "Do you think Tim'll like it?"

"It looks like a piece of wardrobe from a porno shoot. Tim'll love it."

Chelsea let out a girlish giggle. Sometimes it was hard to believe she was also eighteen.

"Talking of Tim, where is he? You two are usually joined at the hip these days."

"That's because he's so gorgeous." She whipped another thong off of the rack. "He's helping a friend of his on some renovation job to earn a little extra money, you know, so he can visit me at college."

College. The real world. Everything was racing towards me at an ever increasing pace, but for some reason I wasn't scared. The thought of leaving home was nerve racking, but at least Chelsea was going to be there with me.

"Do you think you and Tim'll continue, after we're at college?" I'm not sure why I asked. I already knew the answer.

"Probably. Maybe. At least for a while." She paused for a second, her gaze drifting off in to empty space. "Think of all those poor frat boys I'd have to let down. We can't have that now, can we?"

The two of us both giggled at that. It was true though. There would be countless more 'Tims', when we reached college.

After we had finished hunting, Chelsea went to try some things on. All I wanted was to get a nice cool drink, but she insisted it wouldn't take long.

I sat on a sofa that had been put out by the changing rooms and started rifling through a glossy magazine. It seemed like I had been sitting there for all eternity. Several other customers had come and gone in the time Chelsea had been behind the fake wooden door of the changing room. I felt awkward. Out of place.

"Hurry up, Chelsea, it's getting late."

"Almost done."

I knew why she was taking so long. Despite all her grit and flirty ways, underneath she wasn't as confident as she seemed. Deep down she had serious body issues. I caught her once, fingers down her throat up to the knuckles, puking in one of the more secluded bathrooms at school. Of course, she wouldn't admit it. But I knew what it meant.

"There you go, all finished," she announced, as she near enough glided out of the changing room. "Let's go."

She grabbed me by the arm and dragged me off to the cashier's desk. As I stood to one side, a laugh escaped my lips. Nathan had his face squashed up against the pristine glass window. The manageress was trying to shoo him away.

Chelsea walked up beside me, a scowl furrowing her brow. "Why does that geek have to follow you everywhere?"

"Leave him alone. He's a really sweet guy, if you give him a chance."

"He's weird," she replied. "Look at him."

By now the manageress was out there giving him a stern lecture. He was mimicking her posture.

"You can't tell me you two have been friends for like, ever, and not bumped uglies?"

"Eww Chelsea, that's gross. You can be so vulgar sometimes."

"It's part of my charm." She flicked her hair back. "So, have you?"

"You know I haven't."

"Not even a grope?"

"Chelsea, it's not like that with me and Nathan and you know it." She could be so annoying at times, especially if she had a bee in her bonnet about something.

"It just fascinates me how a boy and a girl can be good friends without having sex." She watched him out of the window then began nodding. "He may be a geek, but he ain't bad lookin', girlfriend."

"I don't think of him in that way and neither does he. He's like a..." I couldn't think of the right word. "A brother. Or close cousin."

"And he thinks the same?"

"Of course he does. Sex doesn't have to be an issue."

Chelsea smirked slightly. "If you say so, sweetie."

The manageress had given up lecturing him. He beckoned for the both of us to join him outside by waving his arms around like a madman. He was such a clown back then.

The late afternoon sun dazzled me as we walked in to the street. The crowds were beginning to thin. In the distance, a black silhouette darted across the sky; no doubt a blackbird getting in some hunting before the last good rays of sunlight disappeared for the evening. I don't know why, but Willows Peak gets a lot of blackbirds.

"Wassup, ladies," Nathan said, strolling towards them, his battered old BMX in tow. "What's going on in the hood today?"

Chelsea rolled her eyes. "Stop trying to talk all gangster, moron."

Nathan got down on one knee. "For you my lady..." He took her hand and kissed it. "Anything."

She snatched it back, screwing up her face. "Freak."

"We're off to get a milkshake," I butted in. "Fancy tagging along?"

He grinned from ear to ear. "I'd love to."

The three of us made our way down the street to Fred's Milkshake Bar. I felt like I was at a tennis game, as the banter between Nathan and Chelsea shot back and forth over my head. Nothing nasty. It was all kind hearted. They continued at it all the way down the road, right up until we sat down in our usual booth.

"Fancy splitting a Cherry Surprise?" Nathan asked.

"You know I won't say no to that."

Time seemed to fly past. I can't really remember what we talked about. I remember it being a fun afternoon. Fred's was where everyone used to hang out. Well, until they got their hands on a fake ID, then they migrated to Logan's Bar on the edge of town. I always preferred Fred's.

After an hour had passed, a loud growling erupted outside the door, as a black Ford Falcon skidded to a halt. I could hear Guns and Roses playing *You Could Be Mine* through the frosted window. Chelsea's face lit up. Two rough looking guys walked in, their muscular arms gleaming with sweat.

"Hey Timmy," Chelsea called out. "Over here."

It was a moment I'll probably never forget.

Tim and his buddy made their way through the maze of tables, avoiding the other customers. "Hey baby," he said, squeezing himself into the seat next to her. Without skipping a beat, his tongue slipped straight between her lips. They were like a couple of animals. The other guy just stood there, as if he didn't know what to do.

"My God you two, get a room would'ya!" The one thing I hate is watching couples going at each other. Needless to say, they promptly stopped.

"I told you about that job I'm working on, didn't I, babe?"

"Yep," Chelsea replied.

"Well, this is the guy I've been working with. His name's Justin."

The new guy, Justin, nodded his head in acknowledgement. Up to that point, I hadn't paid much attention to the two of them. I don't think I ever looked away again. The guy was stunning. His brilliant blue eyes pierced in to mine. My heart skipped a beat, as I tried to make it less obvious that I was staring at him. There was something in those eyes that I couldn't pinpoint. He was beautiful. To me, everything about his features was perfect. His skin was a pale, pearlescent white, which contrasted with his jet black hair that was styled, so that one half of his face was covered when his head was bent forward. He also had some light stubble on his chin that framed his strong jaw. His black vest t-shirt was tight across his broad shoulders and chest. I could only imagine that underneath the clothing was a stone solid body. Nobody had ever captured me like he did.

"And you would be?" He reached out a hand towards me. I took it. "I-I'm R-Rachel."

"Pleased to meet you, Rachel."

"Jesus Christ, Rach," Chelsea piped up. "You sound like such a frickin' retard."

Tim was the only one at the table that laughed. To be honest, I'm surprised he came up for air long enough. Even to this day, my cheeks still go red at that memory. That is, when I decide to let myself think about it.

"Well we better get going," Justin said, tapping Tim on the shoulder. Even his voice was mesmerising. "We gotta get to Old Man Marley's hardware store to pick up those supplies before he closes, or my old man will have my balls." He tipped his head towards me. "Pleasure to meet you, Rachel."

I just shot back a dumb smile, as if to say 'likewise'. I couldn't speak. Never, in all my life, had I expected a guy to have that kind of power over me. Part of me was unnerved by the sensation. I tried to ignore it.

Chelsea and Tim finally parted. She was like a kid at Christmas after all the presents had been unwrapped. She turned to me as the door closed. "God, I'm glad I bought that underwear. I think I'm going to need it tonight."

My brain didn't register the part about the underwear. "Where are you going again?" My reasons for asking were more than just curiosity.

"We're going to catch a horror flick at the cinema and

then probably grab a bite to eat at the diner. Why do you ask?"

Nathan had stopped slurping the last dregs of his milkshake. He looked at me with his inquisitive eyes. There's a reason he became a police officer. "Why do you need to know what they're doing tonight? It's Saturday. I usually come over for DVD night."

"I know, but I was hoping we could give it a miss for one night."

He pushed the empty glass away from him across the table. He didn't once look up. "What else did you have in mind?"

"Well," I began, turning to Chelsea. "I was hoping I could go with you and Tim to the cinema."

Chelsea looked puzzled. "Why would you want to come with me and Tim? I thought you hated being the third wheel."

"I was hoping you could ask Tim to bring Justin along with him. You know, make it a foursome." I had never been a forward, or pushy, person in my life. I don't know what came over me. Even Nathan looked bemused.

"So, you like him then?"

"He seems okay. I guess."

Chelsea was over the moon "I was hoping that you would. I'll see what I can do."

She slid out of the booth and rushed out the door. Nathan put his baseball cap on. I'd forgotten he was there.

"You going?" I asked, feeling a little guilty for brushing him off.

"Yeah, Pa'll wonder where I am if I don't get home soon."

"Are you okay about us skipping DVD night?"

"It's cool. I've got things to do anyway. We can do it another time."

"Sure thing."

"Well, have a nice time, pretty lady."

"Bye, Nate."

I watched him wheel his bike down the road, as I sat alone in the booth. There were so many things that we could, and should, have done differently. But we were kids looking to have some fun. What do kids know? Instead of going after him, I sat and waited for Chelsea to return, hoping for an answer that would make my dreams come true.

***

The beginning of the night couldn't have gone any better. As a group we decided to go and see Hitchcock's *Psycho*, which was playing at the cinema on Main Street. The others had seen it, but I hadn't. Not that it mattered to Chelsea anyway; her and Tim spent the majority of the film making out. Justin and I didn't. I sat next to him and shared some popcorn. A few times during the film, I flinched; his strong arm wrapped around my shoulders, letting me know he would protect me. I felt safe with him.

After the film had finished, we spilled out onto Main Street and made our way to the diner. The air was close. There wasn't a single cloud in the sky. The stars sparkled like cat's eyes.

As it was getting late, the diner wasn't very busy. It was one of those fifties diners where the waitresses bring out the food trays on skates. The interior was full of silver seats with red leather covered cushions. There was a jukebox on every table and the walls were adorned with icons of the era; there were the likes of Elvis, Buddy Holly and James Dean watching the customers stuff their faces full of greasy food. It was nice. Fun. We ordered two baskets of cheesy fries to share and a Cola each.

"Where are you guys working again?" I asked, wanting to know more about this stranger that had come into my life.

"We're at that old place up on the hill," Justin replied, taking a handful of fries. "My father bought it for a steal and wants to fix it up. He thinks he can flip it and make a few bucks."

"Do you mean that house made of wood outside town?"

"That's the one. It's an amazing building, with a bucket load of potential. I've been given the job of renovating it while my dad's out of town. It's hard work."

"Since when has drinking beer and getting high been classed as hard work?" Tim butted in through a mouthful of cheese.

"That place gives me the creeps. I've heard the strangest things go on up there. People going missing, ghost sightings, that sort of stuff."

"Ooo, I heard those stories too," Chelsea added. "It's such a sorry sight sitting out there all alone. I think somebody should bulldoze it and build a mall."

"No way," Justin snapped. It was as if he had been personally wronged by her remarks. "There's no way anybody could do that to such a beautiful building. You wait until we've finished fixing it up. You'll soon change your mind then. It's going to look awesome."

At that point he could have swept me off my feet and run away with me. He was so full of passion for his project. It didn't matter how dilapidated, or dead, the building looked; I believed every word he said.

I looked over at him. He was smiling at me. I smiled back, trying to hide my embarrassed cheeks.

"Do you have any brothers, or sisters?" He asked with genuine interest.

It was as if we were having a date on our own; Chelsea and Tim were far too busy with each other to worry about what was going on around them. "No, there's only me."

"I wish I could say the same. I've got an older brother that's a pain in the ass, but I barely see him these days. He's away at college. I've no idea what he's studying."

I sounded like Chelsea, as I let out a tiny girlish giggle. Jesus, I'd have laughed if he told me my hair was on fire.

"Maybe next time we could do this without the gruesome twosome?"

My heart almost leapt out of my mouth. I didn't know what to say. The palms of my hands were soaking. Was he asking me out? My brain just couldn't grasp the concept that this amazing guy wanted to see me again. I stared at him, dumbfounded.

"Are you okay?"

"I-I-I'd love to," I blurted out. He must've thought I was an idiot. "See you again, I mean."

It was his turn to laugh. "Awesome."

We hung around at the diner for at least another hour or so, laughing and joking, swapping stories about how we had grown up in the same sleepy little town. As it turns out, Tim had only met Justin a few weeks beforehand at a car rally in Stockton. He really was a complete stranger. The thing is, it didn't matter. Not to me anyway. By the time we had finished eating and they had driven me home, it felt like I'd known him my whole life. He was so open and honest about everything. It wasn't until my head hit the pillow and I'd drifted off into peaceful slumber that I realised something in me had changed. I had fallen in love.

CHAPTER TEN

Two weeks had passed since we had all gone to the cinema as a group. They were probably the most amazing two weeks of my life. Officials had gone on record to declare it as one of the hottest summers in history. More importantly, I had seen Justin near enough every day since that first meeting. What had started out as a chance introduction by a friend had blossomed into a budding relationship. Of course, I only saw him in the evenings; he spent most of the day working up at the house. To me, looking at it from a distance, it didn't seem any different; still the same forlorn structure that locals tended to stay clear of. Justin insisted they were making steady progress though.

Chelsea came strolling into my bedroom, her wet hair wrapped in a towel. She often stayed over when my parents were away on vacation. It was a good job too. The rest of her was totally nude.

"Will you please put some clothes on, girl," I said, hurling a fluffy yellow pillow at her.

"I like to walk around as the good Lord intended," she replied, throwing the pillow back at me. "Not making you jealous, am I?"

"With *your* chicken legs, no chance."

"Bitch," she replied lovingly.

"You really should put some clothes on though. You never know when Nathan might pop through the window."

"That guy is so annoying. Why do you still let him climb through your window?"

I didn't bother to give her an answer. It wasn't weird to me; it was something we had always done since we were children. I think it's nice how old friends do things that no one else seems to understand. It's what friendship is all about.

Chelsea got dressed. The entire time she kept checking the clock. I realised she was waiting for a call from Tim. She had informed me earlier in the day that he and Justin had gone off to a rally together. I hadn't told her that I already knew because I'd been seeing Justin without her knowledge. She would have gone schizo if I had. She was always one for knowing everybody else's business. My keeping a secret from her would have been seen as a personal vendetta.

She sat down on the bed next to me, crossing her legs. She picked up a pillow and began hugging it, as if it was Tim.

"What do you think the boys are up to?" she asked, lying back on the bed.

"I don't know. Looking at cars, drinking and doing whatever else guys do on those rallies."

"Do you think Tim loves me?"

"How am I supposed to know?" I replied, taken aback by the question. "What makes you ask?" It was totally unlike her to care whether a guy had feelings for her, or not.

"No reason," she said with a sigh.

We lay there for some time looking up at the ceiling. Back then my room was covered with posters of my favourite pop stars, or my favourite movies. I suppose you could say it was a typical teenager's bedroom; a haphazard concoction of trinkets and piles of clothes scattered everywhere. It was my own little cave of wonders.

Chelsea rolled over onto her side facing me. "So," she said, that familiar sly look in her eyes. "What do you think of Justin?"

My breath caught in my throat. Did she know? Maybe Justin had told Tim and then he passed the information on? "He seems okay."

"Just okay? He's absolutely gorgeous. Girl, if I didn't have my man already, I'd be jumping his bones like there's no tomorrow."

"Thanks for the image, Chels."

"I'll have to get you two together again. One meeting

clearly isn't enough."

Justin had kept his promise and said nothing. I don't know why I was so intent on keeping it hidden from the world. It was my secret, no one else's. I coveted my time with him. I didn't even know what it was we had between us. I'd tell her eventually. I guess I just didn't want to jinx anything before it'd been given a chance to begin.

A loud bang at the window announced Nathan's arrival. His spiky gelled hair appeared over the top of the windowsill, followed by his beaming suntanned face. "Howdy folks."

"Hey Nate," I called back over, noticing a flicker of disappointment wash over him as he saw Chelsea next to me. It was gone as quick as it appeared.

His long legs stretched in to the room, as he climbed through the window. His foot stuck. He hopped around and tugged at it, trying to free himself. After one almighty pull it came loose, causing him to trip. He lay face down, sprawled out across my pink shaggy rug. We all laughed.

Time seemed to fly past in my bedroom, as the three of us chatted away the evening. I remember we consumed a lot of pizza, as we laughed and joked together that Friday night. We were happy. Things were as they should be; three teenage friends hanging out, having fun. None of us could've known the terror that was waiting, lurking out there in the dark night. In all honesty, I think it was the last time I felt normal; not sullied by memories and night terrors. It was the last time I felt anything.

The Hello Kitty clock on my bedside table blinked 23:00. Chelsea was by now running out of finger nails to bite.

"For God's sake," I said to her. "He'll phone at some point."

"You can catch diseases from doing that," Nathan added.

"Shut up, Nate," she spat, leaping off of the bed. He went back to surfing through the T.V. channels. "What if something's happened? An accident? Those two are always drinking beer. Anything could've happened to them."

My heart sunk to the pit of my stomach. The thought that

they might be in trouble had never occurred to me. I took a deep breath to clear my head of the sudden fear welling up inside. "They're no doubt just out having fun and Tim's forgotten to call. You know what he's like. I'm sure it's nothing."

"Why don't you call them?" Nathan said, this time not looking away from the T.V.

Chelsea snatched at her cell phone and began dialling, her fingers working the buttons like a woman possessed. She placed it to her ear. A few seconds passed. I sat on the edge of the bed, crossing my fingers behind my back. A few more seconds passed.

"Why isn't he picking up?" Chelsea asked. She had begun to pace around the room like a caged animal.

"Give him a chance, he might be driving."

"It's okay for you, Rach. It's not your boyfriend."

"I -"

Her face was a sudden fury. "For Christ's sake, Tim, where the hell have you been? I've been worried sick."

My heart finally had a chance to stop beating at one hundred kilometres a minute. I let out a sigh of relief under my breath and went to sit on the floor next to Nathan. He had been watching some police chase show on T.V., oblivious to the unfolding drama.

"Sup, Chica?" he asked, as I crossed my legs.

"Nothing much. Chelsea got hold of Tim."

"Shame."

"Hey," I said, giving him a playful slap around the back of the head. "Don't be mean. I thought you liked Tim?"

"I can't stand him. He's a complete and utter douche bag. Guys like that are always bad news and I don't suppose that friend of his is any better. You're better off staying away from them."

"They're harmless, especially Tim. He's too dumb to be anything else."

"And Justin?"

It was a good question, but there was something in the

tone of his voice that caught me off guard. Of course Justin was okay. I'd spent the last two weeks with him. I knew him better than anyone. I was about to give him the full details on how Justin was in fact a nice guy.

"Hey Rach," Chelsea called over. "Justin and Tim have had a brilliant idea. Why don't the four of us spend a night at the house they've been working on?"

"When?"

"Next weekend."

"I'm not so sure, Chelsea. We leave for Fort Kent on the Monday and I want to make sure I'm all ready for that."

"I know, but it'll be our last weekend together as a group," she said, giving me her sad puppy dog eyes. "You've got to come, Rachel. It can be our last hurrah."

"I don't know."

"Pleaseeeee."

"I'm with Rachel on this one. I don't think you should be goin' to the house and stayin' overnight," Nathan added, switching off the T.V. "Do you know how many strange things go on up there? Pa says people go astray all the time. He's got a bucket load of missin' case files, all connected to that house."

"Butt out, Nathan. Who said you were invited?" Chelsea glared at him. If looks could kill, he'd have dropped down dead like a duck on a hunting trip.

"I'm only saying -"

"Well don't!" She turned her attention back to me. "Are you comin', or not?"

I looked from one to the other, not really knowing which way to answer. Nathan's eyes implored me not to say yes. Chelsea's said the opposite. All I could think about was Justin. A whole night together before I left for college.

"I guess it'll be okay."

"Woohoo. I guarantee you won't regret it."

Chelsea turned her attention back to the cell phone to tell the boys that we would be joining them the following weekend. Her face had lit up when I said yes. She was so excited. I knew

I was in for a restless night, but something at the back of my mind was telling me that it wouldn't just be Chelsea keeping me awake.

"I can't believe you're going to go up there with those cretins," Nathan said, walking back towards the window. "Didn't you listen to a word I said? It's seriously dangerous out there. Something is wrong with that place. I mean, *really* wrong with that place. Please tell me you'll change your mind?"

I'd forgotten he was there. "I'm sorry, Nate, I've already said I'd go. And of course I listen to you. Apart from Chelsea, you're my best friend."

"Then don't go."

There was something in his eyes that I couldn't quite put my finger on. I didn't know whether it was concern from a friend, or abject terror. It unnerved me a little. But I wasn't one for breaking plans with friends.

"I'm sorry Nathan, I want to go." A thought struck me. "Why don't you come with us? I'd love it if you did and I'm sure the others won't mind. What d'ya think? It'll be the last chance I get to spend any time with you before I leave for college."

He looked angry. "Screw it. If you won't listen to me, then to hell with the lot of you." He took one last look at me before descending down the ladder. He gave me a look I did recognise. Pain. "Have a nice life." And with that he was gone.

I wanted to go after him, to tell him everything was going to be okay. That he was being ridiculous. But I didn't. I just sat there, watching him slowly fade away out of the window.

Chelsea came bounding up behind me. "Won't it be so awesome, just the four of us up at the house?"

"I guess so," I replied, hearing the words, but not listening to what she was saying.

"You've got to be excited? I know the house isn't much, but you can have fun anywhere if you're with the right crowd. Don't you think so, Rach?"

"Hmm, sure."

"And of course I'll fix you up with Justin. That goes without saying."

"Great. Thanks."

"Oh my God, what's wrong with you?"

Her face looked as though I'd slapped her.

"It's nothing, just something Nathan said. I'm not so sure it's a good idea to be up at that house without anybody knowing where we are. What if something happened to one of the boys? I can't drive and neither can you."

She looked at me, as if I was mad. "That's what cell phones were invented for, dummy." Her face softened, as she took me by the shoulders. "Forget about Nathan. He's just cranky because he knows his Pa will kill him if he found out. He doesn't want to be stuck down here, so he's trying to scare you into not going. You trust me, right?"

"Of course I do."

"Then stop worrying. Nothing is going to happen out there all the time the guys are with us. It's going to be a whole weekend of pure, unadulterated fun. It'll all work out perfectly."

CHAPTER ELEVEN

"It sounds like your friends meant a lot to you," David said, before taking the last bite of his starter.

"They did."

Rachel's mind was whirling with all the memories that had come flowing back to her, as if out of nowhere. Sights, smells, sounds, all things she thought she had long buried, deep within the darkest corners of her mind. The entire time, she hadn't stopped playing with her napkin. David had listened intently, not interrupting, or commenting.

He looked at her, his face gentle and encouraging. "Tell me about your time at the house."

Rachel's fingers worked furiously on the napkin beneath the table. "I don't know if I can." She looked down. "Anyway, there's nothing to tell."

"Okay."

They sat there for several moments, a black void opening up between them. The tall waitress came over with a colleague to remove the empty plates. The restaurant still wasn't too busy, but the atmosphere seemed charged with anticipation.

The waitress informed them the main course would be out shortly and asked if they would like more drinks. David declined. Rachel ordered an Archers and Lemonade. She hoped Becky's night was less stressful.

Outside, the storm had begun to pick up again.

***

Nathan stood in the howling wind, his back leaning against the side of Logan's bar. The vibrant orange glow of a cigarette flickered in and out of life like an awakening demon, as it sat shaking in his right hand. He raised it to his lips and took a drag, the buzz from the nicotine filling his senses. He exhaled the acrid smoke into the damp night air. It had stopped raining. Thank God for small mercies, he thought. There wasn't much else to thank Him for these days.

The argument with David earlier in the evening had left a sour taste in his mouth. Who did that jumped up prick think he was? Nathan thought. If he hurts a hair on her head, I swear to God I'll kill him.

A steady stream of patrons flocked in and out of the bar, as Nathan flicked away the last dregs of his cigarette. The rain hadn't seemed to put off the hardcore drinkers of Willows Peak. Several of them nodded their heads towards him in recognition. Their faces said it all. He may be a deputy sheriff. But he was one of them.

The tip tapping of hurried heels drew his attention down the street. The woman was dashing towards him with an apologetic look on her face.

"I'm so sorry I'm late," Becky said, trying to catch her breath. "We had a bit of an emergency back at the bed-and-breakfast."

"Really? What kind of an emergency?"

"Rachel had one of her panic attacks in the hallway. She -"

"Oh my God, is she okay?" Nathan asked. He looked frightened.

"Okay, calm down, she's fine. She's gone on her date with Doctor Cochrane."

"What were you thinking?" Nathan was practically screaming now. "How could you let her go out after a panic attack?"

"Now you just wait one damn second. I tried to explain to her that I didn't think it was a good idea, but Rachel's a grown woman and I have no right telling her what she can and can't do. And neither do you." Becky turned to walk away. "Maybe this wasn't such a good idea after all."

Nathan gritted his teeth, took a deep breath and calmed his mind.

"Becky, wait, I'm sorry." He jogged to catch up with her.

She spun on her heels. "Why should I? You don't even know me."

"Please, I've had a really rough day."

"Oh, and you think you can take it out on me. Well that's okay then. Screw you, I'm out of here."

"No, wait, please." He grabbed hold of her arm. "That's not what I meant."

She shot him a glance of anger. He let go of her arm.

"Please can we just start over? Let's go inside. I'd really like that."

Becky nodded and allowed Nathan to lead her back to the bar. He felt like such an idiot. It was another example of how easily things got destroyed when it was left up to him.

Inside was like any other typical, honky-tonk bar. At the back end there were a couple of pool tables and a small dance floor, with a few customers dancing to some country music. At the front end, there were a dozen or so tables, most of these taken up by the regulars drinking pints of brown liquid. A bright neon jukebox sat in another corner, mesmerising with its flashing lights. The main feature was the bar itself, stretching across an entire length of wall. Above it sat a yellow sign, *don't touch the women, but they can touch whatever they want to.* Another one read, *leave your troubles at the door unless you want some in here.* Dotted all around the walls were pictures of singers and bands that had, at some time or other, played on a tiny stage just off the dance floor.

Nathan could hardly see in the subdued orange lights of the place, but his instincts allowed him to navigate around the busy tables, avoiding any patrons that might take offence to him bumping into them.

He and Becky sat down on the stalls at the bar.

"Evening, Nate," the brunette barmaid said, giving him a flirtatious smile. She was old enough to be his mother. Grey hairs were starting to surface through her dyed curls. "What can I do for you and the little lady there?"

"Just a bud for me, Gloria."

"Takin' it easy tonight huh, deputy?"

"Something like that."

Gloria laughed and turned to Becky. "What'll it be for you, hun?"

"A white wine for me please."

"Comin' right up."

Nathan's eyes followed Gloria's backside, as she dashed off to get the drinks. He quickly covered up the staring, as he remembered he was on a date. The two of them sat there, waiting for her to come back with the drinks. It was only a few seconds before she returned and then dashed off again to serve some other customers.

Becky took a sip. "This place is amazing. I didn't expect to find a bar like this in the middle of Maine. I feel like I'm in Deep South."

"Yeah, Gloria there's from Texas. Moved up here years ago, opened this place and been here ever since. She's always telling people that she'll go back home one day. She never does though."

"Cool."

They sat sipping at their drinks for a few minutes. Nathan felt awkward. He could count on one hand how many times he had been on a date in his lifetime. And the last one of those had been years ago. Yet another thing he had failed at.

"Do y -"

"I -"

They laughed as they realised they had both been about to say something. Becky motioned for Nathan to go first.

"Look, I'm really sorry about earlier. Rachel's a really good friend of mine and I hate to think of her with problems. And I've had a really rough day. Not that it's an excuse to take it out on you."

"It's okay, I understand. Nothing about this last week has been easy, especially not for Rachel. She's lucky to have a friend like you."

"I don't know about that," he replied, taking another swig of his beer. "I could say the same about you."

"I'm her roommate. It's part of the code."

They both laughed again. Nathan could feel the tension in him start to ease away. This might turn out to be a good evening after all, he thought, looking at the pretty girl sitting in front of him.

The two of them sat chatting for a short time, exchanging stories of their childhoods and the past.

"And so when my Ma died, Rachel was there for me. That's how we became close I guess."

"That's a sweet story," Becky said, drinking the last of her wine.

Nathan noticed she had run out and nodded to the empty glass. "Fancy another?" he asked.

Becky nodded.

He ordered them more drinks. "So," he said, as they waited for Gloria to return. "How much do you know about what went on here?"

"Not much, only that Rachel went through something horrific. She never talks about it."

"Nobody does," Nathan replied, handing over some money.

"I know what you mean. There's something about this town that lurks beneath the surface. You can see it in people's eyes. I guess a big tragedy like that would leave a scar on a small community like this."

"Damn straight."

"What actually happened here, Nate?"

He took a large gulp of the frothy brown beer. His eyes darkened over for a second before he looked back up at her. "Do you want to let me kick your ass at pool?"

"Sure. But I'll be doing the ass kicking."

The unanswered question hung in the air like a dead carcass. Neither one of them mentioned it as they strolled off towards the pool tables.

***

Rachel hadn't realised she'd been fiddling with the locket again. The silver chain felt heavy around her neck. It had left stinging red marks along the white skin where she had been pulling at it. She was beginning to wish she had never thought of going on a date with a psychiatrist. Somehow, he had managed to dredge up all these old emotions from deep within her. Now they hung off her like dead leaves, wilting and rotten. She didn't want to remember. It was too painful.

"David, I don't think I can go on. The memories are just too hard to bear."

He took her by the hand. "That's okay. Maybe we should take a break from talking about the past for a while."

They sat in silence for a few minutes, each of them picking at their food. The restaurant was getting busy. The hum of conversation buzzed around them. Yellow light from the candle flames flickered in the gloom of their little booth. It gave the place a serene atmosphere. Like a church. Rachel noticed Mr and Mrs Krupp arrive, her looking as though she could commit murder with a single look, him forever the dutiful husband. Neither of them paid her any mind, as she tried to duck her head down behind the palm of her hand in order to hide her face. The last thing she wanted to do was make another scene, which inevitably would happen if Mrs Krupp opened her mouth. Now she understood why psychiatrists had offices.

"How's your food?" David asked.

"It's very nice, thank you. How is your steak?"

"Delicious." Blood oozed out of the fleshy meat as he cut.

Rachel was beginning to feel awkward. If the best they could manage were a few lines about the food, then this was going to be a long night. She looked at her watch. It was only half past ten.

"So, do you like living at the bed and breakfast?"

"I did."

"Oh?"

"Sorry, didn't I tell you, I picked up the keys to my new

house yesterday. The renovation isn't quite finished yet, but it's fine for me to move in. I'm going back there tonight."

"At least you don't have to suffer Mrs Ryan anymore."

"Her bark's worse than her bite."

Rachel giggled. The old battle axe wouldn't be giving her any more problems that's for sure.

"Where *is* your new place?"

"Oh, it's just outside town. Why don't you tell me what happened next?"

Rachel put her knife and fork down. She sipped at her drink, ignoring the fact that he had switched the conversation back to her. "There isn't much to tell. What happened can't be changed." She had prayed for that a thousand times over.

"What did happen?"

"I wonder how Becky's date with Nathan is going? He could do with a nice girl like that in his life."

"I think we should keep this about you." He took another bite of his steak. "Tell me more about this Justin. He sounds important."

"I don't want to, if it's all the same to you."

"Why not?"

Rachel was taken aback by the look in David's eyes. There seemed to be a macabre glint in them. It was as if he was enjoying watching her squirm beneath the weight of his questions. It's just your imagination, she tried to tell herself. Whatever she thought she had seen was gone, replaced by his usual warm kindness.

"I'm here to help you, Rachel. You'll only be able to get over your fears if you confront them."

"I know, it's just…" She stopped. The words just didn't seem to want to come out. They were locked inside her. Just like her memories. "I'm sorry, I can't. It's too hard. This was a mistake."

"It's okay. This must be a painful experience for you. It's never easy to face the past especially when it contains something you feel is better off forgetting."

He took hold of her hand. She felt strange. Relax. It was as if, by touching her, he was taking away her fears and doubts. Their eyes locked together. She could melt away in the vastness of those blue pools, she thought, a rare tender smile lighting up her face. For the first time in years, she felt at peace.

"Don't worry," he said. "I won't let anything happen to you. I'll protect you."

A choking lump caught in her throat. She pulled her hand away from his. "What did you say?"

"I said I would protect you. What's wrong with that?"

"I-I-I'm sorry." The stuttering had returned.

"Calm down and take deep breaths."

She did as she was told. David signalled the attention of the waitress and asked her to bring over a glass of water. When the waitress returned, she sipped at the ice cold liquid. She felt numb.

"Now tell me what's wrong."

"You sounded like him."

"Like who? Justin?"

"Yes."

David sat back in his chair. He looked worried.

Deep down Rachel knew she couldn't go on like this. Every second of every minute she was back in town, it would only get worse. Something had opened up inside her. Like Pandora's box, more and more evil would pour from her, never giving her any peace. It had all started when she saw the house coming back into town. It was with her all the time. She knew it was out there, waiting for its next victim. She had to do something about it. Anything.

She looked at the man opposite her. He was strong, dependable. She felt as though she could tell him anything and he would believe her. Maybe if she poured her heart out, she thought, at least someone would know. Maybe they could stop it from happening again?

"Are you ready to tell me the rest of your story?"

"I think so."

"You don't have to if it makes you too uncomfortable. You can stop any time you like."

"I know."

"In that case, why don't you start with the journey up to the house? Tell me about that."

Rachel took another sip of water and then a large gulp of her Archers and Lemonade. She shifted in her seat. Not once did she take her eyes off of the table.

"The group of us drove down in a black Chevy Impala. Tim's pride and joy. It sped along the old dirt track like a panther. The engine growled with exhilaration. None of us knew what was waiting at the top of the hill, or that this would be our last weekend together…"

CHAPTER TWELVE

I peered lazily out of the rear window. The car, going at such a speed, made everything move past my eyes in a blur. The rhythm of the engine hummed along to the sound of AC/DC singing *Highway to Hell*. In the distance, I could see the old white house. As we got closer to the destination, my heart beat faster and faster to the point where it was matching the beat of the song, thundering out of the speakers. I still couldn't quite work out why I had agreed to tag along.

You've got to come, Rachel. It can be our last hurrah.

As true as that was, there were plenty more things that I would rather have been doing before travelling on to college. I really didn't want to be there. Or that's what I kept telling myself.

Despite trying to keep cool, my anxiety was beginning to bubble beneath the surface. It wasn't just because of where we were heading; they were only silly ghost stories. It was the fact that we were speeding down a remote road and Tim had been drinking with Justin before picking us up. The smell of alcohol in the small compartment of the car was intoxicating. My senses were beginning to overload.

"You okay, Rach?" Chelsea asked.

"Yeah I'm okay," I replied, putting on a smile and then turning back to the window. The last thing I wanted to do was spoil the fun by being all prissy. Anyway, it wasn't all bad. Justin was there to hold my hand. This would be the weekend that something would finally happen between the two of us.

Just as the song reached its climax, the car ground to a halt on the driveway. Tim jumped out of the car whooping and shouting like a clown, as Chelsea followed behind him, laughing at his crazy antics. I just sat, gazing out of the window at the big wooden building. It was mesmerising. From a distance, it looked like nothing more than a clapped out old shack. But up close, it was a different story. The house was huge. Decrepit. Most of the old whitewashed paint had chipped away and the old beams holding up the porch roof were weathered with age. Even the eight steps leading up to the door were battered and worn away. In my mind it was the windows that stood out more than anything. In most houses, the windows created pictures of warmth and joy. Here, they were just black, lacking any homely comfort. No curtains, no light. Empty. They were like eyes. Lifeless. To me they seemed sad, devoid of any happy memories. The house just sat there looking out over the countryside, forlorn and hopeless, as if it was waiting for someone to end its misery.

"You planning on joining us, or spending the night here?" asked Justin, giving me his usual playful grin.

I stepped out of the car and on to the driveway. The only sounds were the other three messing around and the gravel of the drive crunching beneath their feet. Apart from that, it was silent. This was a place we shouldn't have been.

My eyes were fixed on the house. "Guys I'm not so sure this is a good idea."

"Stop being so stupid. There's nothing here to worry about. It'll be fun," replied Tim. "Justin, get the beers from the car while I unlock the door."

Justin turned to me and gave me another smile. "Don't worry, I'll protect you."

I returned the smile and made my way up the old wooden steps. My heart pounding with each second. Something wasn't right. I let the others enter the house first and turned around for one final look over the countryside. It was still. Not even the swing stirred in the breeze, as I entered.

***

The musty smell filled my nostrils as soon as I stepped over the threshold. It wasn't the typical smell associated with old homes, where people haven't lived for a while. It was the smell of decay. It was so disgusting, I almost gagged. No house should smell like this, I thought, as I moved further in to the heart of the building.

Lord knows what the guys had been doing up there. No doubt drinking beer, discussing chicks and getting high. That, or not turning up at all. Whatever it was, they hadn't been working.

The entrance opened up in to a room that, at one time, may have been a living room, or parlour. Cobwebs hung low from the ceiling, and I had to bat a curious spider away from my face as I explored. The source of the smell was coming from the damp walls. It had caused the wallpaper to rot and peel away, revealing green mouldy patches. The floorboards creaked with every footstep, as if my weight was causing them distress. There was very little furniture and all of it was covered in a thick layer of dust. The main piece was an old fashioned writing bureau against one wall with a simple wooden chair. The rest consisted of a small coffee table by the front door and a battered old sofa, which had also started rotting some years ago. There was an archway to my left that led to a similarly dreary kitchen and a doorway at the back, which opened on to a corridor. The final pieces of the room were a fireplace that looked like it hadn't been used in centuries and a single, dirt covered window that looked out over the porch and the front garden with its lonely swing. None of it had been touched for years. The decorating materials were all stacked in the corner of the room, waiting to be opened. I was about to say something when I stopped.

Right in front of me was the most striking thing in the room; a portrait of two children with their parents. It had suffered over the years. The young boy's half had been torn, so that his face could no longer be seen. But the girl could be. I assumed it must have been his sister. She was young, but very pretty with jet black curly hair and big brown eyes. There was something about her though. She looked sad.

"Don't worry, you'll get used to it," Justin said, as he

walked past me and put the bags of food and drink on the dining table in the kitchen. Was he talking about the smell, or the picture?

I watched him begin to unpack the bags. Chelsea and Tim were nowhere to be seen, but I could just about make out Chelsea's incessant chatter upstairs. By now, Justin had slotted into our little group perfectly. We were all best buddies. Except I wanted to be more than just friends.

I still hadn't worked out what our relationship was. I didn't even know if we were in one. As soon as I had seen him that first time, I knew I would fall for him, and the more I got to know him, the more I fell. Soon I would be going to college, so it really *was* the last chance I would get to let him know how I felt.

"Umm, do you need a hand?" I enquired.

"I thought you'd never ask," Justin replied, looking back at me.

His blue eyes sparkled in the subdued light. I walked towards him, trying to hide my growing attraction.

"So, having fun yet?" he asked playfully, as he dipped into another bag and started unpacking it.

"Ummm kind of," I replied. I had never been so nervous. I could hear my own heavy breathing. Keep it cool, I thought to myself, as I focused on the bag I was unloading.

"Only kind of? Come on, you love it here." Justin gave me a playful nudge, which sent a surge of heat rushing to my face. My cheeks gained a scarlet tint to them. Did he know how I felt? "Seriously though, do you not want to be here? I can take you home?"

Great! He thinks I'm a wimp, I remember thinking. I really didn't want to be there though. All my senses were screaming at me to take him up on the offer, but I couldn't. If I had left at that point, I would have gone off on the following Monday and probably never again seen the only, genuinely nice guy I had ever met.

"It's not that I don't want to be here, it's just..." I looked around the place and then back to Justin. "You know?"

"I see your point. It's not exactly The Waldorf."

"No it's certainly not," I replied. We were both smiling now at the little joke we had shared. I noticed a glint in his eyes when he smiled at me. I wanted to just fling myself at him, but I also didn't want him to think I was desperate and needy either. God, did I want to be with him though. The only thing that was stopping me was my own irrational fear of rejection. What if he didn't feel the same? I would have looked stupid.

At that moment, Justin took a step closer to me, never once taking his eyes off of mine. My heart thundered. My legs felt like jelly. He took my hands and I was acutely aware of my soaking palms, which were unlike his bone dry ones. He pulled me close.

"You'll be safe. I'll be with you," he whispered.

I didn't know what to say. This was it. My moment. It was as if he had read my mind. His head bent towards mine. I closed my eyes.

The door slammed shut with an almighty bang.

I near jumped out of my skin, letting out a high pitched yelp at the same time. The wind outside was howling a gale. Justin took me by the shoulders.

"It's okay, it's okay," he said, trying to hide his amusement.

"It's not funny." My whole body was shaking. I wanted out. "What the hell was that bang?" My eyes were frantically darting around, trying to find the source of the commotion.

"Look it was just the wind blowing the front door shut." His eyes burned deep inside me, but his ever present smile was reassuring. "There's nothing to be afraid of."

"I know. I'm sorry." I had stopped shaking. The uneasy feeling still hadn't left. It was probably nothing. I had to calm down. I wiped my hands across my face. "I feel so stupid!"

Justin laughed. "Well it could happen to anyone. This place is weird. Even I'm a bit scared. But do you know what's good for fear?" He turned to the table with his back to me then jumped back around. "Wine!" He held out his arm and raised his eyebrows, thrusting the wine bottle under his other arm. "Would madam like to accompany me to the parlour?"

I picked up two glasses and returned with a mock curtsey. "Why certainly, sir."

The two of us made our way back to the living room, avoiding cobwebs as we stepped through the archway. The room had become even darker now, but it wasn't quite night yet.

Tim and Chelsea came bouncing in to the room, Tim with a grin the width of the Hudson and Chelsea wiping the sides of her mouth with a hand.

"Hey don't start without us," Tim said in his deep voice, as he spotted the wine bottle under Justin's arm.

"What was that bang we heard?" Chelsea asked, a hint of anxiety in her voice.

"I told you babe, it was the bogey man come to get you. Mwahaha!"

Tim tickled her until they both collapsed on the ancient sofa, a cloud of dust dispersing in to the air on impact.

"Okay guys, I don't need a live porn show," I said, grabbing Chelsea by the shoulder and pulling her up. "It was just the front door. You and I are going to go freshen up." I gave Chelsea a stern look, which was returned with a look of disappointment in her hazel eyes. A few minutes ago I had been a shaking mess, ready to bolt out the door like a thoroughbred. Now here I was, taking charge of the group.

I wasn't sure what had caused the change in me. I was astonished. I had always been one to sit back and let others take charge. My whole life, I had been pampered and privileged. I'd never needed to take charge of anything. I felt like an adult for the first time in my existence. I guess it was because I wanted to enjoy my last days as a kid and not be afraid anymore. I turned to Justin.

"We won't be long. You can pour me a glass ready for when we get back if you want?" I shot him the most seductive look I could muster.

"Okay, will do," he returned with a wink.

I took one last look at the forlorn portrait hanging above the fireplace. The young girl's eyes stared back at me. There was something, but my mind couldn't grasp it. I pushed it from my thoughts and followed Chelsea deeper in to the bowls of the house.

CHAPTER THIRTEEN

Chelsea led the way up the long narrow staircase with me close behind. Even though my fear of the house had abated, I still didn't want to find myself alone anytime soon. I was walking so close that Chelsea's feathery red hair kept tickling my face. Not that she had noticed how close I was. She was too busy nattering away about how cool Tim was and how he was such a good kisser, at which point I switched off and began to think about my own love life.

I had never really had a proper boyfriend. I'd had boyfriends, but none of the relationships had lasted long. I thought I had loved them, but there was one fundamental problem; I couldn't bring myself to sleep with them. It wasn't that I was shy. I had done other stuff. I was afraid the guys would hurt me. Physically and emotionally. So many times Chelsea had come to me in floods of tears after a guy had dumped her, and each time it was the sex that had made it more complicated. The first time, I even had to help her get the morning after pill. Chelsea's attitude towards sex had become very cavalier and I secretly envied her for that, as I'd finally met a decent guy and I didn't want to lose him.

The upstairs of the house was the same dank and dreary as below. In places, the wallpaper had rotted away, revealing termite infested walls. There was very little light coming through the dirt encrusted windows, but what little that did manage to fight its way through the stains cast sinister shadows across the floorboards. When the last rays of light dipped behind the horizon, I realised we would need torches to see. Chelsea led me in to the first bedroom. There were three in all, two on this floor and one on the top floor, with one bathroom and what would have been a study downstairs with the living room and kitchen.

Chelsea suddenly spun around, making me jump. "Did you bring condoms?" Her face was serious.

"No I did not," I replied, taken aback by the suddenness of the question. "And if I did, who's to say I wouldn't want to use them myself?" That was my way of broaching the subject.

"You?" Chelsea returned, raising her eyebrows and crossing her arms.

"Why not?"

"Because you don't do sex. You never have."

"Well…maybe things have changed." They had, but I wanted to ease in to the subject.

"You're serious aren't you? Ooo, you have to tell me more."

"I like Justin. A lot. I haven't told you, but we've been spending time together, just the two of us. And now…I think I love him."

"You love him?"

It wasn't the reaction I was expecting. No fire balls flew from her eyes. No rivers of blood. The apocalypse I had envisioned at my secret revelation never came.

"He's a nice guy," she continued. "But you barely know him, Rach. Even I don't know him that well."

"I know, but there's something about him. I know he likes me. We almost kissed downstairs, but that damn door stopped us. I felt so stupid."

Chelsea laughed and poked me. "You dumb ass. Well, I'm not going to say don't do it. But think about it first. You don't want to go rushing in to something you'll regret."

"I haven't rushed in to it. Tonight's the night."

And it would be, I thought. With all the alcohol we would be consuming, something was bound to happen. I would wait until Chelsea and Tim disappeared, and they evidently would, then I would make my move. It wasn't the greatest place to be for my first time, but with a few candles it could've even turned out quite romantic.

Chelsea took me by the hands and looked me straight in the eyes. "Promise me you'll be careful." There was genuine concern in her voice.

"I promise. And you too," I replied, giving her a wry smile.

"You know me, baby girl," she said, winking back at me. "Right, I need the toilet. I'll be right back." And with that she left me all alone in the gloom.

It wasn't a huge room, I realised, as I stepped further in to the darkness. From the looks of what was left of the decoration and furniture, it would once have been a child's bedroom. In one corner sat a doll's house, all decked out with dust riddled furniture. The only inhabitants left were the spiders that seemed to infest every room of the house. Along another wall stood a small bed. At the bottom of it lay an old wooden chest which, at some point, would have held the occupant's belongings. I remember wondering what secrets the box used to contain, as I moved around the room. On the wall next to the bed was a single shelf, displaying a collection of four china dolls. Each one had been disfigured in some way. Two had missing eyes, their blank sockets highlighted by their bright smiles. One had no hair, making its smooth skull look oddly cue ball shaped. The final doll had half of its face smashed in, giving it a menacing look. This particular doll's arm was extended out, reaching in to the blackness of the room, as if it was pointing to something. Its single eye bored in to me, imploring that I take a look. The sight caused me to give an involuntary shudder. The room was giving me the creeps, but something was compelling me to follow the arm. Curiosity killed the cat, I thought, as I walked over to the grime encrusted window.

Outside it had finally gone black, as the night set in. I looked out over the countryside, unable to see anything. The woods, the road, the blank fields. All of it was out there somewhere, under the darkness. I realised how far away we were from any form of civilisation.

In space, no one can hear you scream.

The tagline popped in to my head, as I looked for signs of life. We weren't in space, but I certainly doubted anyone would hear us if we were to scream. Chelsea seemed to be taking ages. The thought made the uneasiness I had felt earlier creep back in. To calm my nerves, I stared at my reflection in the window pane.

I had always considered myself to be a plain looking girl. Green eyes, a short, sharp nose, a few freckles and thin lips with perfect straight teeth. My hair was in a ponytail, pencil black in colour. When I was younger, the kids at school used to make fun of me, until Chelsea hit one, knocking out two teeth. They never did it again, but I still hadn't been that popular. I guess that was the real reason why I was still a virgin.

"What the hell?" I said, more to myself than anyone in particular.

Outside, staring straight at me, was the young girl from the portrait. She was standing by the swing. Her white dress had a red circular stain in the middle. I blinked and rubbed my eyes, thinking that I was seeing things. As I looked closer the girl was half smiling and half snarling. I shot from the room.

"Guys, guys, come quick," I hollered down the corridor.

Chelsea came out from the bathroom. "What is it, hun? What's wrong?"

"The girl. The girl from the portrait is outside."

"What portrait?"

"The one in the living room. We have to get out of here."

"Calm down Rach and stop being ridiculous. There are no such things as ghosts. You're just seeing things."

The guys came bounding up the stairs, Justin in the lead. He looked at us. "What's going on? We heard shouting."

"Rach thinks she saw something outside. A girl, or something."

I noticed the hint of annoyance in Chelsea's voice.

"I saw her!"

"Saw who?" Justin asked gently, looking straight at me.

"I saw the young girl from the portrait in the living room.

She was standing right by the swing. Go take a look for yourselves."

Justin, Chelsea and Tim moved to the window. A few moments passed before Justin turned back. "There's nothing there, Rach."

"Told you," added Chelsea, raising her eyebrows.

"But I saw her."

Justin came over to me and took my hand. He led me over to the window and pointed out. "See, just the tree and the swing."

"But…"

"For the love of God Rach, there's nothing there. Come on Tim. Let's get this party started."

And with that, Chelsea led a cheering Tim out the room and back down the stairs. For the second time that day, I was left alone with Justin. Whatever I had seen was gone now. But the face of the girl was still vivid in my memory. Justin continued to hold my hand. He had such a calming influence.

"Don't worry. Your imagination is bound to play tricks on you in a creepy old house like this."

"I saw something Justin, I know I did."

"It was probably kids. We're not the only people around here. Mr and Mrs Clarke live just around the next hill. Their grandkids are always playing pranks up here."

The explanation seemed to sound genuine. I didn't have anything else better to explain what I'd seen out in the darkness. It was reasonable to agree with his suggestion. I could feel my pulse slowing and my mind becoming more rational.

"You must think I'm an idiot," I said, looking at the floor.

He lifted my head and looked into my eyes. "Not at all. In fact I think you're cute."

I was lost in the overwhelming sense of strength that his gaze gave me. A minute passed, then another. Or that's what it felt like. In reality, it was seconds. But I had gone further than that. I could see a bright future with just me and him. Nothing else mattered. I've never wanted anything more than I wanted him in those passing moments.

"While we're alone," he said, reaching in to his back pocket. "I want to give you something."

My heart had picked up speed again.

"It was my Grandmother's."

Dangling in front of my face was a beautiful silver locket. I felt hypnotised, as it spun on its chain, every now and then winking like a star every time the faint light caught the smooth surface.

"I can't accept this."

"Don't you like it?"

"Oh no, it's beautiful," I replied. "But it's too much."

Justin smiled. "Let me put it on. I want you to have it."

He gently placed it around my neck. My senses were filled with him. It was intoxicating to the point where it was making my head spin.

"It suits you," he said stepping back.

"Thank you so much. I'll never take it off, I promise."

Then I kissed him, overtaken by an impulse. I'll never forget. It was a long sweet kiss that made my body tingle. He obviously felt the same, as he kissed me back. I noticed his lips were dry, but firm, as his tongue explored my mouth. I could tell he had done this before. Our lips parted leaving me wanting more.

He looked down, fidgeting on his feet. "That was unexpected."

"I'm sorry if I got-"

"No, no, I liked it." He looked up, placing a hand on my burning cheek. "It was a nice surprise."

We just giggled together before kissing again, all inhibitions gone. The second time was even more amazing than the first, without the nervousness acting like an invisible barrier between us. Playful screams pulled us apart.

"Shall we go join the others?" he asked. "We don't want them starting without us."

"Okay."

Justin led me back to the rest of the group. I had almost

forgotten the incident at the window.

CHAPTER FOURTEEN

"Wow, a kiss. That must've been a special moment for you?"

"It was my first real kiss," Rachel replied, the sensation of his lips lingering on her mouth with the memory.

There was never a day went by where she didn't think about it, or remember how wonderful she felt at that moment. A first kiss is something a girl always remembers, she thought, trying to hide her sadness. Everything in her life seemed so simple back then. All she had to worry about was the usual teenage angst that everyone goes through. Now it felt like the world was on her shoulders. So much had changed.

"Have you and Nathan ever kissed?"

"No, why do you ask?"

"You two seem very close. It would be natural for two young people that close, to experiment, especially when they're of the opposite sex."

"Nathan and I *are* close, but not in that way. We've been friends for far too long to let something like that get in the way. If it didn't work out and I lost him as a friend, I would be devastated."

"I see."

The thought of Nathan made her think about Becky. They were out on the town somewhere. Rachel had never known two people who were more suited to each other than her friends. She just hoped they realised it as well.

***

The sickly yellow lights reflected off of the filth stained white tiles, making the small men's room look brighter than it actually was. The stench of urine wafted around the room, permeating every nook and cranny. The walls that weren't covered in dirt were instead covered with posters of semi-naked women clinging to the wall. Seductive eyes stared out at the male patrons relieving themselves after filling their bladders with destructive liquids.

Nathan stood over one of the urinals, leaning his weight on his left hand against the wall. So far, so good. After his bad start to the evening, he could finally feel the tension in his neck and shoulders stating to subside. Thank God, he thought. He wasn't sure if he could continue much longer. There was too much temptation around him. He could feel the familiar gnawing at the back of his brain, urging him on.

Go on. One more. One more can't hurt.

No, he thought. Tonight he had to fight it. There could be no giving in.

He zipped his blue jeans up and walked over to the sink. After washing his hands, he splashed the harsh cold water on his face. He stared intently at himself in the cracked bathroom mirror, one hand on the sink. The crack ran the length of his face. His eyes, haunted and weary. He hated it, the control it had over him, the things it made him do. All of it. Like a relentless wolf hunting its prey, the desire to appease the addiction never left him. There was a lot of pressure on him to sort himself out, which didn't help; his Pa was the sheriff, how could he not assume he would be able to escape the weight of expectation to hang heavy on his shoulders? It was an impossible situation.

He continued to stare hard at himself. People laughed at him behind his back, he knew that much. Coward, that's what they called him. Weak. A good for nothing drunk, that'll no doubt kill himself one day. Maybe he would, he thought. But not before he'd shown them all what he was capable of.

A clatter behind him caught his attention.

"Evenin', deputy," a grizzled old man said, as he waddled over to the urinals.

"Stanley," Nathan replied, heading towards the door.

"Mighty fine lady, ya got yerself out there. Why, I reckon

she's prettier than all the flowers in the sweet Lord's garden."

"You might be right there."

"I know I am, young'un. Fine pool hustler too," he added with a wink.

Nathan laughed. "Damn straight."

"You keep a hold of that one, Nate. Mighty fine woman."

"I will," he said, turning to leave.

The old man's words had struck something inside him. It felt as though a torch had been shone on a dark part of his soul and scared away the spiders. Becky was on a date with him because she wanted to be, nobody had made her. She didn't know his past, or any of the things people said about him. Not yet anyway. But none of that mattered anymore. She was his chance for a fresh start. Redemption.

He stopped, halfway out the door. "Thanks, Stan."

Then he left.

Becky was still sitting by the bar where he had left her. He sat back beside her.

"You look pleased with yourself," she said, raising an eyebrow.

"Do I?" Nathan replied.

"Yeah."

"Must be the good company I'm keepin' these days."

He caught the appreciative glimmer in her eyes, as she realised he was talking about her. She really does have pretty eyes, he thought, watching her over the top of his beer glass. Any thoughts of Rachel had been pushed from his mind.

"So," Becky said, lowering her glass. "Tell me more about you."

He gulped at his beer. "Not much to tell really."

"There must be something. You grew up here, right?"

"Yep."

"What was it like back then?"

Nathan put his empty glass next to hers on the bar and cleared his throat. "Willows Peak hasn't really ever changed all that much. It's always been a sleepy town stretched out on some back road off the main route. Everybody knows everybody else's business. Merryville is the only other town nearby."

"I've heard of it. Wasn't it on the news a while back?"

"It's always on the news. Don't get me wrong, we've got our own fair share of oddballs, but the folks are damn crazy up there."

Becky let out a giggle. To Nathan it sounded nervous.

"I'm sure they're just rumours," he added.

The two of them chatted a while longer, exchanging stories of their pasts. Friendships, school, embarrassing moments. All of it came under scrutiny. But for the first time in over a year, Nathan was enjoying himself. For too long he had been trapped in a cycle of guilt and self-loathing, mixed with a garnish of regret. Not anymore. He was finally breaking free.

"Rachel never talks about her life here," Becky said, turning a napkin over between her fingers. "I mean, she's told me what happened at the house, but only snippets. Whatever happened, it's terrified her right down to her bone marrow."

Nathan's jaw clenched, the Masseter muscle pulsating.

"She wakes, screaming sometimes."

"Sure."

"What really happened out there, Nate? You're her friend, has she ever said anything to you?"

"I don't know what happened," he lied. "I wasn't there and she was shipped off to college three days later. I hadn't seen, or spoken to her since then, until the other day."

"I just wish there was something I could do."

Nothing more was said on the subject. Nathan was glad, but now he couldn't shift the thought of Rachel, out on a date with David, from his mind. He needed a distraction. Or *it* would start calling again.

"Fancy another game of pool?" he asked.

"Yeah, sure."

"Cool. I'm going out for a cigarette, so rack 'em up and I'll be back."

"Sure, you want another butt whipping?"

"No chance."

As he walked away, he took a look at the whiskey bottles stacked behind the bar. He licked the sweat from his top lip and walked out.

***

Rachel was glad the conversation had steered clear of her past and anything connected to the house. For a while at least. She couldn't dodge it forever, she knew that much. But since mentioning the kiss, David hadn't pushed her at all. If anything, he'd gone in the opposite direction, she thought, taking a sip of water. He had led the conversation, steering them around casual topics and away from talk of the house. Maybe he had heard enough? She wondered. It suited her just fine.

She gazed at him as he spoke. There was still that feeling of familiarity deep inside her. Still, she couldn't put her finger on what it was about him that she felt she had known before. His speech, his mannerisms, even his eyes had something that seemed so recognisable and yet, so very different. He had a quirky charm about him. One that had made her feel at ease from the very first moment they met. She put it down to the fact that he was a psychiatrist; they always know how to handle people, it's part of their job. But this was something more. In a strange kind of way, it excited her. She liked it.

"David," she blurted out, cutting off his speech. "I need you to be honest with me and answer a question for me. Are you sure we haven't met before?"

He laughed. "No, definitely not. You asked me that earlier."

"I know, but there's something about you. It all sounds crazy, but I feel like I know you somehow."

"What, like a past life?"

"Now you're just making fun of me."

He adjusted his tie. "Honest I'm not. Don't you believe in that kind of thing? The supernatural and all, I mean?"

Rachel sat back in her chair and thought about it for a moment. When she was younger, her parents used to make her go to church on a Sunday morning. The preacher had been some greasy fat man that ended up being thrown in jail for inappropriate relations with young boys. She hadn't any other experiences with religion, or the supernatural. The real world was scary enough. She knew that first-hand.

"No, I don't think I do," she replied.

"I didn't think you would. You're not the type."

She was intrigued. "Oh really, and what type am I?"

"Well, you seem like a well-grounded kind of person. I mean, you're majoring in Behavioural Science, correct?"

"Yes."

"That means you probably have an inquisitive mind, but also an empirical one. You need cold hard facts, rather than conjecture. You also don't seem like the kind of girl that does things on a whim."

"I'm here, aren't I?" Rachel said with a cheeky grin.

"Nobody said psychoanalysis is an exact science."

They both laughed at that. She could feel the air around her becoming lighter without the stench of the past clinging to them.

Despite beginning to enjoy herself, the image of the house standing there on the desolate hillside sat firmly in the forefront of her mind. She wished she knew who had rebuilt the damn thing. If it wasn't there, then she might have been able to enjoy her time being home. Despite the circumstances of her return.

She missed her parents deeply. The thought of never seeing them again, hearing their voices, smelling her mother's perfume, overwhelmed her. But then she remembered how they had been with her since that night. She could remember their faces. They had shown no care, or concern. Only fear. They had been afraid of what the neighbours might think, or that their precious membership to the yachting club might be withdrawn because they had a crazy daughter. Damaged, she'd heard her mother call her the night before they shipped her off to college. She had hardly spoken to them since then; a phone call, a birthday card and a visit at Christmas was all. How could she feel aggrieved after they had shunted her off to somewhere at the other end of the state not wanting to be associated with her? But still, the loss bit deep into her heart.

"Are you okay, Rachel?" David asked.

"I was just thinking about my parents." She hadn't meant to tell him. It had just spurted out.

"I never had the chance to tell you how sorry I am for your loss. I never met them, but I've heard they were well respected members of the community. You must miss them a lot?"

"I guess so."

"Have the police managed to get any further with the investigation?"

"No. They're pretty certain there was no foul play involved."

"Well, I suppose that's a good thing. If -"

"Can we change the subject, please?" she cut in.

"Of course, if that's what you want."

She regretted snapping at him as soon as the words had left her mouth. He was being so kind and sweet to her. She wanted to make it up to him, but she didn't know how. Apologising had never been her strong point.

"I didn't mean to snap at you. I'm sorry, it's just my parents, I haven't had much to do with them since I left town. In fact, it was them that encouraged me to go."

"Please, don't worry about it. I fully understand what you must be going through. The loss of a close family member, especially a parent, is always a hard thing. Maybe it's time we got back to the reason we're here?"

The inevitable had arrived. It dawned on her that he had been leading them back to the subject all along. He was good. She had to admit that.

"I guess we could."

"You can stop any time you feel it's getting too much. I'm here for you."

She knew he meant it too. She could see it in his eyes.

"Thank you."

"It's what I'm here for. I'm ready when you are."

She took a deep breath and cleared her mind.

"We were having a good time after the kiss. None of us had a care in the world. I guess at that age it's how a group of teenagers should be on their last weekend together. Carefree. Somehow, even the house seemed less gloomy and oppressive. I should've known it wouldn't stay that way…"

CHAPTER FIFTEEN

The group of us had been partying for over an hour, with most of the alcohol already gone. I felt as though I was viewing the world through glasses that were way too strong for me; I had only drunk a few vodkas, but it was far more than I could handle. Chelsea, who had drunk nearly a bottle of wine, was fine. Justin had been by my side the entire time.

I could still feel the lingering traces of the kiss on my lips. My heart hammered in my chest every time I thought about it. I was in love, there was no denying that, but the fact that I would be leaving for college the other side of the state, tainted it. Long distance relationships never really work. It wasn't just leaving Justin that made me feel down. I looked around the dank room. It was becoming more and more of a paradise by the minute. Chelsea and Tim were at each other again; every now and then she would let out a girlish giggle signalling her enjoyment. Apart from that, and the crackling flames of the fire, everything was quiet. It was perfect.

"What's up?" Justin asked, wrapping his arm around my shoulders.

"Nothing, I'm fine."

"Can't fool me," he said, with a nudge. "I hope it wasn't the kiss upstairs?"

"No, don't think that. It's just..." I let the sentence trail off. Should I tell him? I fretted. Should I pour my heart out?

"You can tell me."

"I just don't want to say goodbye to everyone. My friends are all I've ever had. Well, them, and a credit card as a parent."

Justin laughed at my feeble attempt at humour, stroking my hair and smiling at me. "Try not to think about it. Nobody can predict what might be around the corner."

"I guess you're right."

"I'm always right," he replied, smiling like a Cheshire cat. "I'm getting a drink, you want one?"

I thought about it for a moment. "No, thank you. I think I've drunk enough."

"Go on, one more."

"I can't, I think I'm already drunk."

"Then one more won't hurt," Tim said. "You're always so prissy. Lighten up will ya."

"Shut up Tim!" I retorted, shooting him a look of annoyance. He was right though, I did need to stop being so stiff. "Okay, just one more. But not too much." I didn't want to puke in front of him.

Justin smiled and shot off into the kitchen. Chelsea stood up and then adjusted her skirt. She looked in my direction, tipping me a wink, before grabbing Tim's hand and leading him to the doorway. I quickly caught on.

"Don't go yet," I hissed. "I don't know what I'm doing."

"You'll be fine, don't worry. Have fun." Then they were gone, leaving me alone in the room.

The light from the small fire made the shadows in the room look as though they were doing some kind of macabre dance around the battered walls each time the flames flickered. For the second time that day, I found my gaze drawn to the portrait. The family sitting there looked so happy. But the mother's eyes gave her away. They seemed to have a deep rooted sadness in them.

I sat staring at the picture for several moments, my eyes following the contours of the faces looking back at me. Slowly rising to my feet, I wandered over to get a closer look. Not once did I blink. My eyes were locked on to the girl. The only sound was my heartbeat filling my ears.

"It's amazing that picture has survived all this damp."

The voice made me spin on my heels with a start. Justin was standing there watching, two drinks in his hand. How long had he been standing there? I hadn't heard his footsteps.

He walked over and handed me one of the glasses, his blue eyes encouraging. "Do you know the story of this place?" he asked, walking past me towards the portrait.

"Ummm, kind of." I didn't really know it. All I knew was that a lot of accidents happened there.

"I thought everyone knew the stories. Want me to tell you?"

"Okay."

The two of us sat down on the moth eaten sofa. I sat close, so that Justin could put his arm around me. He took a sip of his drink before starting his tale.

"This old house was built in the eighteen-hundreds by a farmer that owned the fields around the hill. He did it for his family."

"Is that them in the picture?"

"Yeah, I think so." He looked at my drink. "You drinking that?"

I took a large sip, the coke fizzing on my tongue. "So, what happened to them?"

"Well everything started off fine for the first ten years. The farm was doing well, money was pouring in and Mrs McCain had given birth to a fine, healthy boy in that time. Then it all went wrong."

I hung on every word. How did Justin know all this stuff? I guessed his father had told him, what with being the owner and all. I snuggled closer to his chest while I listened to more of the sad tale.

"Mrs McCain eventually gave birth to a daughter. At first, everyone was happy, but after a time a cloud settled over the house. The crops failed, which made the money dry up. The story goes that Mr McCain took to drinking and Mrs McCain had become a recluse after the birth of Lilly."

"That poor family," I said, taking another sip of my drink. I just couldn't believe how a person's life could go from heaven to hell so quick. There was one question I had to ask. "What happened to the kids?"

"You sure you want to know?"

"Yes."

There was an intense pleasure behind Justin's eyes. He looked as though he was enjoying making me hang on his every word. I found my chest rising and falling in rapid bursts.

"Well the story goes that one day Mr McCain came home blind drunk. Jacob, the son, was pushing his little sister on her swing outside."

I shuddered, the image of the girl standing next to the swing flashed through my mind. Justin must have noticed my discomfort. He pulled me tighter to him, before continuing. He had a knack of making me feel safe.

"Mr McCain entered the house only to find his wife dead. She had committed suicide while the children had been playing."

I took more of my drink. I wasn't sure if I wanted to hear the rest, but I didn't have the heart to say anything.

Justin continued, his eyes growing wider. "Without saying a word, the farmer reached for his hunting rifle. Life would be unbearable. He shot himself at point blank range. The locals claimed the shot rang out over the valley like thunder."

I drank the last dregs of my drink.

"Want another one?" Justin asked.

"I want to hear the rest of the story first." I had to know what happened.

Justin grinned. "Well I need a drink. Be right back."

He shot off, back into the kitchen, leaving me frustrated. My head was spinning with the mixture of alcohol and questions. Why were we here? Had I really seen someone out of the window? What happened to the two children? I stood up and moved towards the kitchen. The picture caught my attention, as I moved closer to it.

My breath caught in my throat. No, it couldn't be, could it? I could feel the panic rising again. Stop being an idiot, I thought, trying to quell my rising doubt. The familiarity between the girl in the picture and whatever I thought I had seen upstairs was uncanny. It was just the drink playing tricks on me, I was sure of it. I would've looked like a complete idiot if I'd starting telling everyone that I had seen a girl from a portrait, that was way over a hundred years old. All I wanted was to be with Justin and have a good time.

I wandered over to the kitchen to see if he needed a hand. The two glasses that we had been using were sitting on the table alone; Justin was nowhere to be seen. He must have gone to the toilet, I mused, as I cleared away. God knows why I was bothering; the place was a bomb site. Upstairs I could hear a lot of bumps and people moving around, which I assumed was Chelsea and Tim doing their thing. At least somebody was getting some!

I walked over to one of the grime stained windows. It was completely black over the valley; the only trees I could see were the ones closest to the house. They looked like statuesque guards, watching over the road leading up to the house, swaying in the wind that was picking up to a gale, its maniacal howl whipping through the cracks in the walls. The whole setting looked like something out of a nightmare. I desperately hoped that the morning wouldn't be too long in coming.

On the way back to the living room, I stopped dead in my tracks. The piercing scream filled the house, causing my stomach to drop. The dread that had been rising in me all night became real. I felt sick. That wasn't the wind howling.

"Oh my God," I whispered, bolting for the stairs.

***

I ran as fast as I could towards the sound of the scream. My heart was racing, the blood pumping a loud beat in my ears. I had known all along that something bad was going to happen to one of us; no one had ever stayed in the house without somebody coming to some sort of harm. People had died here. Nathan tried to warn me. I remember praying as hard as I could that it was nothing serious.

When I reached the top of the stairs, Chelsea was huddled

in one corner of the hallway opposite the bathroom, her head tucked between her knees. She was rocking backwards and forwards.

"No, no, no it can't be."

"Chelsea what happened?" I asked, running over to her. "Where's Tim?"

"He just went to the bathroom. He was gone ages. I was waiting for him, but he never came back. No, oh my God, no."

"Chelsea you need to calm down. Where's Tim?"

Still she continued to babble. I shook her violently by the shoulders. Justin came bounding up the stairs.

"What the hell's happened here? Is she okay?" He asked, a look of concern mixed with fear on his face.

"I don't know. She won't stop. Please Justin, try and find Tim. All I could get out of her was that he went to the bathroom."

"Okay, I'll check."

Justin dashed off to the bathroom, calling out Tim's name. I heard no answer, so I just sat, attempting to calm my friend down. She sobbed hard into her lap. God knows what had happened, but I vouched we wouldn't be staying much longer; as soon as Justin found Tim, we would be getting the hell out and never coming back. With any luck, I hoped, Tim would've just passed out in the toilet due to drinking too much. But then why was Chelsea crying?

"Rach, come quick," Justin called from inside the bathroom.

I left her to rock back and forth and made my way there. With every step I took, the fear inside me rose like hot air. The walls seemed to close in on me; the corridor appeared longer than I remembered. Justin stood in the doorway, a grim look plastered over his face.

"Don't go in there," he urged, trying to block the entrance.

I ignored him and pushed past, a morbid need to see for myself overpowering my better judgement. I took a sharp breath then puked.

Tim's lifeless body swung limply on a rope, attached to an exposed beam in the ceiling, a puddle of blood gathering beneath his feet. His eyes had been gouged out and his lips cut in to a permanent smile. His chest looked like a tiger had been playing games on it. Behind the body was a dripping message scrawled in blood along the wall.

Get out! Get out! Get out!

Justin just about caught me before I fainted.

"Are you alright?"

"I told you this place isn't right." Tears started to form under my eyes, the sobs tumbled from my body. The shock had drained me. "I told you I saw something, but no one would listen. N-N-Now Tim's dead."

The two of us stood there for a few moments, surrounded by the horror until I managed to compose myself a little. "We have to call the police."

"And say what? A ghost murdered our friend? No, we'd just be laughed at. Anyway, there's no signal out here."

"What the hell are we going to do?" I screamed at him, letting my fear take control. All I could see in my mind was the doll's face. Tim reminded me of them. "It was the girl, the one from the picture, she did this!"

"You need to calm down and get a grip," Justin explained, taking me by the shoulders. "Go downstairs and get the car started, I'll get Chelsea. We need to get out of here as fast as we can, then we can figure out what to tell the cops."

I stopped crying and looked deep in to his eyes. He was so brave and strong. His strength calmed me to the point where everything felt like a dream, even though I knew it wasn't. I was glad he was here.

"Rachel, go," Justin said, snapping me out of my thoughts.

I did as I was told and made my way back downstairs, listening to my friend's sobs coming from the bedroom. Nothing seemed real. Anytime now I would wake up to the sunshine pouring through my bedroom window, my mother calling me from the kitchen as she cooked bacon and eggs.

I pinched my arm at the bottom of the stairs. Nothing happened; still I was stuck in a nightmare that I thought would never end.

If it was possible, the house seemed colder, darker than it had before. Every shadow, every creak could have been dangerous to me. I had never felt so frightened in all my life, as I approached the front door. I put out my hand, turned the knob to open it.

It wouldn't move. I turned it again. Still nothing. My breath was coming out in bursts, my heart hammering hard against the prison of my chest. I couldn't budge it, no matter how hard I pushed and pulled at it. The relentless howling of the wind continued through the hills, adding its horrific chorus to the nature of the night. My fists pounded as hard as they could, but the door just rattled in its rotting frame. We were trapped.

I dashed over to a nearby window to see if anything had blown in front of the door, blocking off the exit.

Standing next to the swing was a small girl, her jet black hair blowing wildly in the wind, giving it a life of its own. There was no mistaking it this time. It was the girl from the picture, her lifeless eyes staring straight at me. She was pointing to the upstairs. The ghost of Lilly had sealed off the house, only for us to become her playthings; that was until she decided she no longer wanted us.

Several moments passed before I could even think about moving; my brain had shut down from everything that was happening. When my body did decide to move, I ran for the stairs to tell Justin that we were trapped. The sight of the girl, and our current predicament, had calmed my nerves. Our fate was sealed, it was just a matter of time before we were all dead. There's something about the inevitable that makes it easy to accept. Especially when it involves death.

Chelsea must have stopped crying.

"Justin, we're -"

The sentence was cut short. Just as I thought the night couldn't bring any more horrors, I found that I was wrong.

Standing in front of me was Justin. My eyes moved down over him, the dread rising in me like bile. In one hand he had a long curved knife that dripped with blood.

"What's happened?" I asked, the words catching in my throat. "Where did you find that?"

Justin didn't answer.

"Where's Chelsea?"

Still no answer came from him, only a faint guttural breathing. Then I forced myself to look to his other hand. My fear grew with every passing inch. First I saw curls. Soft, red curls matted and knotted. Then I saw the eyes. They were rolled back leaving just the whites visible. I realised with a choked sob that he held Chelsea's head in his blood soaked fist.

I looked at him. His face was twisted in a malevolent grin, drool dripping from one corner of his mouth. An insane glow shone from his eyes like that of a wild animal, trapped behind a cage.

"Hello sugar pie, having a good time? Don't be afraid, the fun is just beginning."

I gathered my senses and ran back the way I had come, my feet thundering down the stairs. Behind me, I could still hear the crazy laughing of the only other person left in the house. I had no idea what had happened to him, or if he had killed Tim as well. And Lilly. What part did she have to play in the unfolding drama?

Thoughts raced around my mind as if it was a race track. I didn't have time to ponder the answers; I could hear Justin coming for me, humming the tune to *Make 'Em Laugh*. There was no doubt in my mind that he had gone totally mad.

I was determined to get out this time. I took a quick look out of the window, but no one was there. The humming was getting closer. I picked up a chair.

"Ready, or not, here I come."

Without thinking, I launched the old wooden chair, riddled with termites and years of decay, at the window. It splintered into pieces on impact, but so did the glass. I was free.

Not wasting any time I clambered through the makeshift exit, cutting my hands and knees in the process. Justin was right behind me, but I was out of his reach.

"Run, Rach, run," he shouted. "You won't get far. I'll find you and bring you back. Then the real party can start."

I ignored his wild howls, as the strong gusts of wind battered my frightened body. Tears streaked down my cheeks. I didn't take any notice. I ran as fast as I could down the track that had turned from dust in to a thick slippery mud in the heavy rain. There was only one place I could stay hidden.

CHAPTER SIXTEEN

"That's it. Nothing more," Rachel said, her entire body shaking, sweat dripping down her spine. "I can't do this, it's too much."

"They're only memories. They can't hurt you anymore."

"I know, David, but I won't do it. I can't do. It hurts too much."

He put down his knife and fork neatly next to the plate of half eaten food. He shook his head.

"But Rachel," he said, a grin widening across his face, as his eyes fixed on her. "The party is just getting started."

"What did you say?" The words tumbled from Rachel's mouth, the whites of her eyes gleaming with terror. She wanted to run, but couldn't move. "Tell me what you said."

"I said," David replied, sitting back in his chair. "You were just getting started. In my pr -"

"No you didn't. That's not it."

"What do you mean?"

Rachel's mind was spinning like a carousel. "You said the party's just getting started."

He looked puzzled. "Excuse me?"

"You did," she was getting agitated. "I heard you say it."

"Why do you think I would say that? What I was about to say, is that in my professional opinion, it's best to finish the story. All the memories have been dragged up already, so not finishing your story could be even more detrimental to you than bottling everything up inside."

She didn't know what to believe. David seemed so genuine, his features soft and concerned. Had she heard him say those words? Was it her mind? All her instincts were screaming at her to leave. But something was holding her back. She doubted herself too much to be certain. It wasn't the first time since she had been home that her mind had sent her reeling through the dark corridors of her memory. If she hadn't heard those words from David's lips, then where had they come from?

"I'm not going on anymore. Things are getting too weird for me."

"But Rachel, you're doing so well. I really think that you should try and continue. It's for the best."

"Best for who? It might be for you, with your case files and conferences, where you can use me as an example of a freak. But it's not for me."

"That's not why I'm here with you tonight. Surely you know that?"

"I don't know what to think. Why are you so interested in this anyway? It's not like you lived here back then, or knew anybody involved."

David fidgeted in his seat, his hand fumbling with his tie. He cleared his throat. "I, err, ummm...I don't really know what to say."

That makes two of us, Rachel thought. Up until now, it hadn't even crossed her mind as to why a complete stranger wanted to help her out. "Go on, why are you so interested in me?"

Again, he cleared his throat. "In all honesty, you intrigued me. I have to admit that after I saw you at the bed and breakfast, I went to the hospital and checked the files. I ran your name through the system and your case was still there. I read through and didn't know what to make of it, so I thought that it would be interesting to get a first-hand account of what happened." He lowered his eyes to the table, as if he was trying to avoid eye contact. "I'm sorry, I should never have agreed to this. My professional curiosity got the better of me."

Rachel was astounded at the audacity of it. The whole time she thought she had been out on a date with a guy that was genuinely interested in her. Instead, it was nothing but a game to him; something to take back to the office and make a name for himself. That couldn't be the only reason, she thought. Could it? She wanted to know, but didn't know how to ask. She sat there, the food on the table going cold. Just like her heart.

"Look," David said, shattering the awkward silence. "If you want to go home, leave this with me and I'll settle up. I didn't mean to hurt you."

She felt as though she could cry. "How could you do this to me?"

"I honestly didn't mean to. I thought I could help you at the same time as learning something from you."

"But I thought you liked me."

This time it was his turn to look shocked. "Are you trying to tell me that you wanted this to be a date?"

Her cheeks flushed red. "Kind of."

"Well," he replied. "I'm flattered. I didn't know that was your intention."

"I guess we both got the wrong idea tonight then."

She wanted to get out of the restaurant. It felt as though a million eyes were on her, boring into the back of her skull. How could she have been such an idiot? It didn't explain away the fact that her trust had been broken by someone that was supposedly trying to help her. She felt betrayed. It was a feeling she knew all too well.

"Whatever tonight may have been, you still lied to me about your reasons for agreeing to this. Why didn't you tell me that you'd looked into my file?"

"I don't know. I suppose a part of me didn't want to tell you because I like you and wanted this to be a date too. I thought you would think it unprofessional of me asking you out after having only just met you."

"You have a funny way of showing that you like someone. I think you need to work on your people skills a bit more."

She felt slightly better after hearing the revelation that he did like her. She could tell that he was being genuine. For the last ten minutes, he hadn't even been able to make eye contact with her. In a way, it was sweet. Screwed up, she thought. But sweet.

"I'm sorry if I was a bit heavy-handed with you." His cheeks flushed. "You make me nervous."

She started to feel herself sympathising with him. "I make you nervous? How is that possible?"

"I haven't been around women since…" David's eyes fell back to the table.

"What's wrong?"

"It's just…I haven't been on a date since my ex-girlfriend. That was a few years ago now."

"Oh really? Why did you break up?"

He pushed the food around on his plate with the fork. "It doesn't matter."

Rachel didn't want to push it, but now she found herself intrigued. Maybe this was the thing about him that she kept picking up on? If she knew all his secrets, then maybe she would find it easier to talk about her own.

"Please tell me."

He looked up. There was a deep sadness in his eyes. "She died when we were in our second year at college. Suicide. That's when I decided to switch my major to clinical psychology. I wanted to help people like her, so that nobody had to go through what I went through. You remind me of her."

She didn't know how to reply to that. Now she understood why he wanted to help her. In a way, it made her feel awkward. She wasn't sure she liked being compared to a dead person. But her heart went out to him. She knew what it was like to lose someone she loved.

She stroked his hand. "David, I'm so sorry to hear that."

"I'm just going to pop to the toilet. I'll be back in a second."

He pulled his hand back from her, stood up and walked away, leaving Rachel sitting alone at the table. She felt terrible. Sometimes, she tended to forget that she wasn't the only person in the world to have a past that she wanted to escape.

She mulled over the facts in her head. The girl had obviously meant a lot to him and although he had broken all the confidentiality rules she could think of, he'd only been trying to help because she reminded him of his ex-girlfriend. And it had been thrown back in his face. Damn, she thought. If only she had known all of it sooner, then she never would've gotten funny with him.

Footsteps behind her said he was back. She waited until he was sat down.

"David, please forgive me. I understand now that you're only trying to help me."

"That's okay. I should've been more honest with you from the start."

He gave her a warm smile that melted away any reservations she still had about him. There wasn't anybody in the world, that she could remember, who could wipe away all her doubts with a simple smile. She returned it.

"You're very cute when you smile."

"You're not so bad yourself. That is, when you're being honest with me."

They both chuckled. It changed the atmosphere around them. The air didn't feel so oppressive and tense any more. There was a sparkle in his eye. She couldn't resist him anymore. A sudden impulse overcame her senses. She lent forward towards him. Her heart fluttered like the beating wings of a butterfly. She felt like she could do anything.

As they kissed for the first time, it felt as though the whole world had come to a standstill around them. She could hear people from a nearby table tutting at their display of affection, as her tongue felt the dry softness of his mouth. It had been a long time since she had acted on a whim. She could feel the gentle pressure of him kissing her back. Nothing else mattered to her except this one moment. For the second time in her life, a kiss had changed everything. It felt so familiar and yet so different. She could trust him with anything. She knew that now.

After a few seconds they parted, adjusting themselves,

realising that people had been watching.

"Well, I wasn't expecting that."

She felt nervous. "Is that a good or bad thing?"

"From where I'm sitting, it's a good thing," David replied.

For the next fifteen minutes, the two of them sat idly talking about everything except the subject that Rachel knew would come around again. She was trying as hard as she could to avoid it, but it hung between them like a foul stench.

"David, about my problem, I -"

"Please, don't feel like you have to continue. We can just enjoy the meal and talk about other things if you want."

She thought about it for a moment. "Is that what you think we should do?"

"It's not about what I want, or think. It's you that has to relive the memories. The pain, the feelings, all of it. Memories can be harder than living it the first time. But remember, we're here for your benefit. As hard as it is to face your fears, if you tackle them head-on, it can be a very rewarding experience. Talking can set you free."

"Is that what you did?" she asked. "I mean, when your ex passed away."

"Yes."

As they finished off their main course, she thought about whether she could continue or not. Last time she tried any kind of therapy, it ended up a disaster and she never went back. David seemed so certain that it would help her. She believed his words. One of the hardest parts was over, talking about the kiss with Justin. Sometimes, she could still taste him. Smell him. Feel his cold breath on her neck. He was the reason no one ever got close to her. Now here she was again, allowing someone to get close. Despite the terror from that night, it came down to one factor; she was afraid of getting her heart broken again. That had affected her more than anything.

If she continued her tale, there was no guarantee that she would be able to finish it. The worst was yet to come. The man opposite her may have read up on her case, but he had no idea of the horrors that she was about to tell him. She took a deep breath.

"The rain pelted at me," she started.

David crossed his hands in his lap, focusing all his attention on her. "Go on."

"I ran headlong in to the woods, the heavy drops slapping against the leaves as they lashed down from the sky. With the trees and the dense black clouds that had slid overhead, I could barely see a hand in front of my face, let alone anything else…"

CHAPTER SEVENTEEN

Every now and then a crack of moonlight peeked through the clouds. I used whatever light there was as best as I could to navigate a route around the hidden obstacles; trees, roots all waiting like macabre ghouls to delay my escape. I tried to block out the image of my dead friends, concentrating on getting away, moving faster than I ever had in my life. The terror propelled me forwards. I felt my lungs could burst at any minute. Running all night wasn't an option.

An unseen branch made me trip. I stumbled several feet, before crashing with a dull thud into a mammoth tree trunk. I screamed, bouncing off and landing in a heap on the floor. The pain in my shoulder was overwhelming.

I dragged myself through the mud and settled between the gaps of a gnarled old trunk. Cradling my arm, I sucked some much needed air in to my lungs. Every breath I took, a stabbing pain shot down my arm; I was pretty sure my shoulder was dislocated.

My brain couldn't focus, as my body was racked with trembles. Not from the damp night air, but from the fear. I had no idea what to do. My instincts screamed at me to run. But I couldn't. My arm throbbed every time I moved the slightest inch. Then there was *him*. Justin was out there somewhere, hiding, hunting me like an animal through the trees. I could feel him; see his face in my mind's eye. That face, twisted and satanic, was carved behind my eyelids. He had been enjoying it. I had seen it in his eyes. What'd happened to him? I wondered, tears finally forming. Had he been possessed? If so, by who, or what? He had been so sweet and gentle. Surely a person couldn't act that way if deep inside them they're psychotic.

Could they? The night was supposed to have been so special. A dream. Instead, it had turned in to a nightmare. One I didn't know how to wake up from.

I let the tears fall, the last of my courage evaporating from my battered body. The reek of decay from the rotten leaves filled my nostrils, as I huddled alone beneath the branches. With my chin tucked between my knees, I rocked back and forth. It was the smell of death. As long as I live, I'll never forget that stench. The place is riddled with it.

I don't know how long the sobs lasted. I didn't dare cry too hard in case he crept up on me. My ears listened for the slightest sound of him being near; a broken twig, breathing, that maniacal laughter. Anything. But there was nothing. Maybe he had given up? I prayed to God that he had.

Wiping my eyes, I tried to stand. My shoulder exploded in to excruciating pain, as I moved. Vomit bubbled up my throat. Like molten lava, it erupted from my mouth, choking me at the same time. I let it come. In a way it was like a cleansing of my soul. My shoulder still hurt, but my thoughts seemed more coherent. It was as if the pain had focussed my mind, cleared away the fog of terror smothering it. I knew I had to do something.

Slowly I crept deeper in to the woods, my eyes and ears alert to any approaching danger. It was silent. Not a thing moved. It was as if the woods were watching; waiting for something to happen. It felt oppressive. Suffocating. I could feel my pulse quickening, my head becoming fuzzy. I stopped to compose myself again.

A sudden sound to my left caused me to jerk my head around. There was nothing. I stood rooted to the spot. My eyes wide.

Then again behind me.
Nothing.
"Who's there?"
No answer.
"Come out, you sick bastard," I spat, my body shaking. "I'm not afraid of you."

Still there was no answer. Was it the fear, I wondered, making me hear things? I didn't know, but I also knew it was dangerous to stay in one spot for too long.

I moved deeper in to the woods with no plan and no idea which direction I was heading. I had this idea that if I kept moving forward, I would stumble across a farm, a town, something that would mean I was safe. But deep down, I knew it was an impossible task in the scarce moonlight under the trees. Still I moved forward.

It didn't take me long to reach a small clearing. A rusted iron fence ringed the edges. It was no larger than two body widths. I took a sharp gasp, as the clouds parted, illuminating the sight.

It was a graveyard. Four headstones stared back at me, ravaged by time. The two furthest away dwarfed the two smaller gravestones closest to the entrance. The weather and plant life had eaten in to the granite, but still they stood. Reminders of the dead. My curiosity had got the better of me, long before I realised I had walked through the gap where the iron gate would have once stood.

I don't know what possessed me to go in there. I guess it was because it was a strange sight, four simple graves sitting in the middle of dense woodland. It was surreal.

My feet drifted forward, towards the nearest grave. My hand trembled, as I rested it on the headstone.

Here layeth Lilly McCain. Beloved daughter of Hiram and Rose McCain. Now and forever an angel.

My eyes followed the curves of the words carved in to the stone before moving to the next one.

Here layeth Jacob McCain. Beloved son of Hiram and Rose McCain. Now and forever an angel.

My brain whirled. It was the graves of the two McCain children. The other two must have been the parents. I couldn't believe it. Sadness overwhelmed me. They had died at the hands of a madman. Did their spirits still remain? I wondered. It wasn't until then that I realised the evil that infested the building looming in the distance. It had permeated the very ground, waiting for its next victim. I was determined it wouldn't be me.

I turned to leave. Staring straight at me was a blackbird, sitting on the fence.

My eyes followed it, as it unfurled its wings and hopped on to an overhanging branch. It sat there, its black eyes looking down on me. I narrowed my gaze, bewildered by the sight. I felt like I was drifting through a dream. I didn't know what was real and what wasn't. I couldn't take my eyes away from it. All the pain and terror I had felt was gone, lost in the past. I felt like I was sinking. Was this what it felt like to be hypnotized? I mused. I could've easily lost myself in those black, void like eyes.

As I stood there, a faint humming began to grow louder in the distance.

My eyes still fixed on the bird.

Louder.

I couldn't move.

Something was getting closer.

It cawed, flapped its wings, pushing itself into the air.

The road!

I ran as fast as I could in the direction of the car coming along the old track at the bottom of the hill. I was saved.

***

I don't know what propelled me forward down the hill. Twigs scratched at my face as I ran. Several times, I lost my footing, slipping through the mix of dead leaves and mud. My legs were getting heavier, caked with slime from each time that I fell over. The pain in my shoulder was almost unbearable. But it didn't matter. I was saved. Why hadn't I thought of the road sooner?

As I stumbled to the bottom of the hill, the rain had turned the road into a river. It was torrential now. The drops were hitting the tarmac so hard, it gave the illusion that the rain was going up rather than coming down. I could hear the car coming around the bend. It would be here in a second, I hoped.

I never even considered how I would stop it. The lights appeared around the corner, coming straight at me. It was moving fast. I didn't stop to think, as I ran into the middle of the road, waving my arms around like a crazy fan at a rock concert. It didn't seem to stop. I waved harder. They were getting closer. I shut my eyes, wrapping my arms around me for protection. This is it. After everything that had happened, I was going to be mowed down by a car.

The screeching filled my ears, as the tyres screamed the car around me(?), trying as hard as they could to gain a firm grip of the slippery surface beneath them. I held my breath, waiting for the impact. It never came.

As I opened my eyes, I saw the car was actually a small truck. The driver door opened.

"What in the blazes do ya think you're doin'?" the old man shouted at me. "Ya could've got yaself killed."

I ran straight to him. The tension built up inside of me behind the dam I had erected finally released the pressure, as I flung myself at him. Sobs shook my body.

"Hey now, miss. What's wrong? What ya doing out here this late at night anyhows?"

"The house...My friends...Dead...He...Justin." The words wouldn't form sentences. I couldn't think straight. Apparently it happens a lot in stressful situations. All I could do was cry into his chest.

"Now, now miss, calm down." The old guy's grizzled hands took me firmly by the shoulders. I winced as he pressed too hard on my dislocated joint. He looked straight into my face. He was full of concern. "I think we best get ya in the truck before ya catch your death o' cold."

I allowed him to lead me back to his truck. He opened the passenger door, sat me in the seat and then closed me inside. The rain tapped a drum beat on the roof. It was coming down so hard, I couldn't see anything out of the windows. We may as well have been underwater. I could feel my eyelids becoming heavy. The heat in the compartment mixed with the sound on the roof was enough to send anyone to sleep. I wanted to let it take me.

The driver's door flew open.

"I'm goin' to get ya to a hospital," the old man said. "We ain't far from town. Why, you're lucky my wife forgot the dog food, or you'd be-"

The words stopped. I looked at my saviour. He just stood there, his eyes gradually growing wider. He went to say something. All that came out of his mouth was a bubbling, frothy torrent of blood. I stared, my mind too tired to understand what was going on.

"Hello, Rachel," Justin said, pulling the dead body out of the way. A bloodied knife dripped onto the fabric of the driver's seat. "You've been a very naughty girl. I'm going to have to punish you."

I screamed.

As I scrambled for the door, he thrust at my face with a knife. A burning sting slashed its way along my cheek, as the tip broke through the surface. I didn't stop to take any notice.

The door flew open and I bolted for the woods. The entire time he was laughing.

"Come on, Rachel. We're just having fun. You can run all you like. I know this place better than anyone and there's nowhere you can hide."

The words echoed in my ears, as I ran headlong back into the dark.

**

I knew he was following me, his relentless cackle filtering through the sound of the rain hitting the foliage. I wanted it to end. Nothing in my life had ever seemed so endless. It was as if I was in a place where time moved backwards, rather than forwards. My body wanted to give in. But I couldn't. How could I let him take me now, knowing what he had done. People had to know the truth.

All I could think about was the dead. First Tim, then Chelsea. And now that poor old man. His face, as he realised he was dying, kept popping into my vision. It had to end.

Before I realised it, the trees overhead had cleared. I had run so fast, I hadn't realised what direction, or for how long I had been running. The silent house sat in front of me. I had come full circle back up the hill. It was as if it had drawn me to it. The dark windows seemed even more menacing than they had when I first arrived. It felt as though they were laughing at me, mocking me for my stupidity. There was no escaping this place. Better to face the inevitable.

A loud ringing filled the night air. Something in my pocket vibrated.

In all the terror, I had totally forgotten about my cell phone. There it was ringing, as if nothing else had happened. I don't know whether it was fear, but the normalcy of it made me chuckle.

I reached into my pocket and pulled it out. It was Nathan.

I pressed the answer button. "Oh my God, I..."

The words trailed off, and the phone dropped to the floor.

"Hello," the young girl said, the bright red stain on her dress more visible this close up. "It doesn't hurt."

"W-w-what doesn't hurt?"

Lilly slowly raised her hand, pointing behind me.

The last thing I could remember, was the butt of the knife slamming down on my head.

"Sweet dreams, sugar pie."

I hit the floor. Then nothing.

CHAPTER EIGHTEEN

"There has to be more to it than that," David said, eating his last morsel of food. "What happened after that?"

"Please, don't make me do any more. I can't remember much else."

"We've already had this conversation. It's better for you to finish."

Rachel just sat there. It was beginning to feel like a tug of war with him. Why wouldn't he just take no for an answer? It wasn't as if it was life, or death. Not anymore. It was in the past and best left there. The clock on the wall said it was almost eleven o'clock. She needed a breather.

"I've just got to go to the ladies' room."

"Okay. I'll be right here when you get back."

She didn't know whether to be comforted, or afraid by his words. There was something in them. Did she detect a hint of threat? Ignoring it, she made her way to the bathroom.

The bright fluorescent lights dazzled her, as they twinkled off the perfectly white tiles lining the walls. She sighed as she bent over the sink and looked at herself in the mirror.

Things were becoming far too complicated with David wanting to know every little detail about memories from a night that had long ago been forgotten. She didn't want to relive it. Once was more than enough. But he was relentless. There was no way she was going to be able to go back to the table and *not* finish her story. She knew he was only trying to help her, but there was something else. Every now and again there would be something familiar about him: a look, a gesture, words. Something that made her feel as though she had seen it all before. But it was impossible. They had never met before the other day.

She sighed again, splashing water over her face. She pushed the thoughts to the rear of her mind. It was best to get back, have dessert and finish her story. Once it was finished she could forget it for good. It would finally be over. Then maybe she could pursue other things with him.

As she let the bathroom door close behind her, she hoped Nathan and Becky were having a better time than she was.

***

Much to Nathan's surprise, he and Becky were having a great time. The loud clash of the pool balls filled the air each time a shot was taken. It was the fifth game he had lost in a row.

"Man," he said, leaning against the cue. "I suck at this game."

Becky gave him a pat on the back, a wry grin on her face. "Not bad for a girl, huh?"

"Guess not."

For the last hour, he hadn't thought about anything other than enjoying the night. He deserved it. It had been a long time since he'd been in the place without wanting to drown his sorrows. In such a short time, the girl kicking his ass at pool had managed to achieve more than councillors, medication and alcohol had achieved put together. The weight no longer hung heavy around his neck.

"Fancy another beer?" Becky asked, placing her cue back on its rack.

"Ummm."

"Go on, one more won't hurt."

It might, he thought. "Okay, I guess one more'll be fine."

They walked over to the busy bar and ordered a couple of drinks. Nathan was beginning to wonder whether it really was his present company lifting his spirits. He had already been drunk before meeting her, but managed to compose himself. Now he could feel that familiar numbness creeping its way back into him; a dulling of the senses, a clouding of his vision. Maybe he should slow down a bit? He contemplated. He knew he wouldn't.

"Can I ask you something, Nate?"

He put his beer glass down. "Go for it."

"When you were younger, did you have a thing for Rachel?"

Rachel again. Why did it always come back to her? No matter how hard he tried to run, he couldn't get away.

"No, not really."

"Are you sure? It's just..." Becky let the sentence trail off. "You know what, forget it. It's stupid."

"No, go on. What was you going to say?" Nathan asked.

"It's just, when I mentioned that she'd gone on a date with David, you seemed to get really jealous. I noticed it the other day at the bed and breakfast as well."

Nathan laughed. "Don't be ridiculous. She's just a friend. I don't want to see her getting hurt, that's all. Our beloved Doctor Cochrane isn't all he's cracked up to be."

"What do you mean?"

"Let's just say, he has a few skeletons in his closet. And I don't mean the kind that they practice on in medical school."

"He seems nice enough to me," Becky said.

Nathan took a huge gulp of his beer. The glass was already half empty. "Anyway, I don't have any feelings for Rachel." He jumped down off his bar stool. "Do you fancy going for a walk?"

"In this weather? I don't think so."

"It's getting really stuffy in here." He pulled at his t-shirt collar. "Don't you think?"

"I hadn't really noticed." Becky gave him a concerned look. "Are you alright?"

"Yeah, yeah, I'm peachy."

"Okay, well I'm going to go to the bathroom. Maybe you should get some fresh air?"

"That's a great idea. I'll do that."

Before Becky could even say another word, Nathan had staggered off in the direction of the door.

The cold air hit him full in the face, as he wobbled over to a nearby bench. At least it had stopped raining, he thought. He breathed in deeply, hoping to get rid of some cobwebs. He had to stop. Bad things always happened when he was drunk. It had been drink that had screwed his life up in the first place. If he hadn't been on it that day the call came in about the shooting, then things might be different. He had let himself down. He had let the department down. If his father hadn't been the sheriff, then he probably wouldn't even have a job. It had taken him a long time to prove to his Pa that he could do it and that he was over it. Ever since then he had been living a lie. One that was getting harder to cover up. Everything was going perfect so far with Becky, he didn't want to blow it with her. Not now.

Usually, he was a functioning drunk. Somebody that could pass themselves off as sober, even if they were so inebriated that the world felt like it was spinning around them. But for just a minute, he had felt like losing control, letting everything go. Just like his father used to when he was a kid. He came home from school one day, his mother black and blue. When he had asked what was wrong, she'd told him Daddy had got mad, but Mummy had deserved it. They said alcoholism was genetic. Maybe it was? He thought. But he would never let it get that bad. He prayed he would never let it get that bad.

***

Nathan closed the front door as quietly as he could. He wanted to smash it, to pretend it was that guy Justin's head. He hated him for taking Rachel away. They had all gone up to the house and left him. He had watched them leave, hiding himself away in the bushes. His blood had boiled over to the point where he had gone and sat in the park, the blackbirds his only company. Rachel was his. She had always been his, ever since his Ma had passed away. He couldn't think of a single moment in the time when she had ignored his advice. It stunk. They can all go to hell, he thought, going deeper into the hallway.

It was always dark in his house. The lights hurt his Pa's eyes, especially if he'd had one beer too many. No doubt he was passed out on the sofa right now, he realised. His ears strained, listening for the low growl of drunken snores. It was silent.

Maybe he was still at work? He thought, his fingers crossed behind his back. He had been lucky once before. But he could never be too careful. It wasn't a good idea to make his Pa angry, not at this time of night.

He stood there for a few moments, waiting for a sound. There wasn't one. Not wanting to tempt fate, he kept his footfalls light on the shaggy rug that stretched the length of the hallway. His hands were trembling. The fading bruises on his back felt raw again, as if they remembered what happened the last time he broke curfew. That had been a trip to the ER. *Fell down the stairs, didn't you? Stupid boy, never looks where he's going, Doc.* Nathan had seen the doctor's face; knowing and yet powerless to offer any form of salvation. He'd seen it so many times before with his Ma. Mr Ross is a respected member of the community, Nathan realised. No one will ever stand up to him.

His feet stopped, before climbing the short staircase. He had to be sure. There was still no sound, no light. Nothing. He let his building anxiety subside.

One step.

He has to still be at work.

Two steps.

Three steps.

Thank God for small mercies.

"Why are you late?"

The deep voice made his blood run cold. His Pa had been skulking in the kitchen all along. Waiting like a predator. Every instinct Nathan had was screaming at him to bolt up the stairs, jam his bedroom door shut and sit tight until the storm passed. But he couldn't move. All he could do was stand there and wait for the onslaught.

"I asked you a question, boy. Why are you late?"

"I-I -"

"Are you a retard?"

Nathan could smell the alcoholic fumes coming towards him. "N-No."

"Then stop stuttering," his Pa said, keeping his voice

level.

He was on the bottom step now. Nathan could hear him undoing his belt buckle.

"I'll give you one last chance, son. Why are you late?"

"I-I'm sorry, Pa. It won't happen again, I promise."

"You may be eighteen, but you live under my roof. My rules."

Nathan still couldn't see anything, as he stepped backwards up the stairs. His Pa was within striking distance. The smell of yeast on his breath was so strong, it almost made Nathan gag.

"Your mother used to make promises that she knew she wouldn't keep. You know what I did to help her keep them?"

Something inside Nathan woke up.

"Don't you dare talk about Ma. I know what you did. She gave you everything and you treated her like dirt, beating her like a dog until she killed herself. Well you won't break me."

"Wanna bet?"

He felt the sting of leather bite into the exposed flesh on his arm, milliseconds before the sound of the slap filled the hallway. Then another. And another. Several missed, as he dodged side to side. He was too angry to be afraid now. He kicked his leg up in the direction of the smell. A grunt, followed by several dull thuds in quick succession announced that he had knocked his Pa down the stairs.

Had he killed him? He wondered. He hated his father with a passion, but he was still his blood and Nathan was no murderer. He stopped for a few moments. No, he was alive. Soft murmurs hovered up to his ears. He bolted to his room.

Locking the door, he dragged his dresser across to act like an extra barrier, before slumping down to the floor, his head tucked between his knees. He felt sick. He clutched at his arms to stop them from shaking. No doubt it was the adrenaline, he realised. He had never stood up to his Pa, no one had. It was the strangest feeling; full of victory and yet poisoned by a dull sadness. If only he had stood up to him sooner, then maybe his Ma would still be around. They would be a family.

Time slipped past. He had no idea how long he had been sat there. The last thing he had heard from downstairs was the fridge door opening and then an audible chink of glass bottles. He obviously wasn't hurt bad, Nathan realised. For an instant, he wasn't sure whether he was happy about it, or not. There was only one person he could talk to. He didn't care if it interrupted her or not.

He reached into his pocket and pulled out his cell phone. He dialled Rachel's number. It rung a couple of times before she picked up.

"Oh my God Nathan, I…"

Then it went dead.

"Hello, Rachel. You there? Rach, pick up."

Nothing.

"Rach?"

His stomach dropped.

"RACHEL!"

***

It was the last time Nathan's Pa ever touched him. And one of his last memories of Rachel. He turned his eyes up to the sky. Everything in his past was entwined with hers. He was sick of it, tired of the memories and of people asking him about her. Yes, he had loved her, but this was the second time she had chosen someone else over him. It was time to move on.

The fresh air had done some good. He stood up, feeling a lot steadier on his feet. He took one more deep breath, letting it out slowly. Then he returned to the bar.

He saw Becky sitting down at a table. He gave her a smile.

"You feeling better now?" she asked.

"Much better. Not sure what came over me."

"We can call it a night if you want? I can make my own way home."

Nathan gave her a serious look. "Look missy, you've beaten me five games in a row. Do you really think I'm going to let you go that easily?"

She laughed. "Fancy another whooping, do ya?"

"From you, anytime."

He watched her as she strolled off towards the pool table, her hips swaying from side to side. He could feel a familiar stirring in his trousers. She looked over her shoulder and gave him a cheeky wink. Time to let go of the past, he thought. Time to let go of Rachel.

***

"The part in the woods sounds like a harrowing experience," David said. "Shall we take a break for a second?"

"Please," Rachel said, sitting herself back down.

She was glad that was over. Her experience in the woods had haunted her every night since. She was also glad that they were taking a short break. She could feel her hands trembling underneath the table. It was awful, having to relive it all; David was right, remembering *was* almost as bad as going through it the first time. The further she got through her story, the harder it was getting. She hadn't even got to the worst part yet.

Despite the storm, the air in the restaurant seemed stifling. Every now and again, she would have to wipe the sweat forming on her forehead.

"I'm just going to visit the ladies' room again," she said.

"Is everything okay? You've only just been."

"Yeah, I'm fine. I think I've left my cell phone in there."

"If the waitress comes shall I order you a coffee, or anything?" David asked.

"Not for me thank you. I'll be back in a tick."

Rachel walked off in the direction of the ladies' room again, leaving David alone at the table. She hated lying, but she needed to clear her head, calm her nerves down. She felt like an idiot. They were only memories, how could she still be afraid after all this time? She thought. The house was rebuilt, big deal. It wasn't as if the house could hurt her. It had been Justin. And he was dead. The dead can't hurt anyone.

The bright lights of the bathroom dazzled her, as she stepped inside again. She took a quick look around to make sure there was nobody else, ducking down low to look beneath the cubicle doors. It was deserted. She took a deep breath and walked over to the counter.

The harsh cold water burst from the tap with a hiss. She put her hands underneath and splashed it on to her warm face. Her eyelids felt heavy. Forcing them open, she took a long hard look in the mirror. What had happened to the girl she used to be? She wondered. Had she died up at the house? Physically, she looked no different, three years older, but that was all. Mentally, it was like two different people. She used to be loving, caring and open to the possibility of an exciting future. Full of life. Now she was cold and hard like granite. Maybe after tonight, after exorcising her demons, she could get back to the way she used to be. But first she had to face her biggest fear. Facing Justin for one last time.

Her make-up had run from the water on her face. Black lines had started to smear down her cheeks. She wiped them with her hands and then opened up her purse to take out her eyeliner.

"Shit," she said, as the black cylinder fell to the floor.

She bent down to pick it up.

"Tee hee."

Rachel stood bolt upright. The child's laugh had come from one of the cubicles.

"Who's there?" she called out.

Silence.

"Come on, I heard you."

There was still no answer. Must've been my imagination, she thought, turning back to the mirror. She had checked every cubicle, and there had been no one there. Stop being so stupid, she thought. There's nothing here.

She blinked. For a second she thought she'd seen a familiar face hovering over her shoulder, smiling. Lilly. But it couldn't be. It was just the stress, she kept telling herself. She prayed to God that she wasn't losing her mind.

"Tee hee."

She whipped her head around.

"Come out, whoever's doing that. It's not funny."

She was becoming scared now. The fear was crawling up her spine, numbing her. A cold breeze brushed along the back of her shoulders. She spun around again. Nothing. What the hell's going on? She thought.

"Tee hee."

The toilet door flew open, as a group of women walked in, giggling and screaming. They looked at her with contemptuous eyes.

Rachel grabbed her bag and flew from the toilet. She needed to get out. Not just out of the bathroom, but out of the restaurant, the town. Being home was the worst place she could be. Except back at the house. She would finish her story and then get the hell out of there. She owed it to herself to finish after getting this far.

David stood up, as she reached the table.

"What happened? You look like you've seen a ghost."

The phrase struck her as odd. Had it been a figment of her imagination caused by stress, or had she actually seen a ghost? She didn't believe in ghosts.

"It's nothing, I'm just tired."

She sat back down. This was it, the hardest part to relive. If she couldn't get through this next part, then she may as well pick up the fork on the table and jab it through her eye socket and into her brain. If she couldn't be fixed, she thought, then life wasn't worth living.

"I'm ready to continue," she said.

David sipped at his coffee, before placing it on the table. "Are you sure?"

"Positive."

"Okay."

She started to fiddle with the locket. "After he hit me, the world seemed to go black. I could hear everything, feel everything, but I was in a different place. Every now and then I would feel a sharp tug at my hair, or a sharp stone slice along my back, as he dragged me along the drive and in to the house…"

CHAPTER NINETEEN

The house had grown cold and silent, the final embers in the fireplace dead. The inside was pitch black without the roaring flames to give off its warm, orange glow. I couldn't see a thing, as he dragged my body along the hard wooden floor towards the living room. Not that my eyes would focus anyway; I was still dazed and confused from the sudden blow to the back of my head. I could feel a thin trickle of blood running down the nape of my neck. My body groaned as I felt his firm grip lift me up and throw me on to the sofa.

I heard his feet shuffle over towards the fireplace. I didn't move. I couldn't. The pain in my body mixed with the fear had almost paralysed me. What was he going to do with me? I wondered. An un-numbered amount of scenarios ran through my head. Maybe this was a prank? Any minute now, Chelsea and Tim would jump out and scream, gotcha! The image of Justin standing there, with the severed head of my best friend, flashed in my mind; her flowing red locks marred by the blood that had tangled the strands together; her eyes rolled back in to the skull; her face stuck forever in a twisted scream. No. This was real. I was trapped in the middle of nowhere with a guy that was clearly out of his mind. What was he going to do to me?

I lay on the sofa, focusing on the steady rise and fall of my chest, trying to block out the pain. I tried to move my legs a few inches, so as not to alert his attention. It hurt, but not unbearably so.

The sound of liquid pouring and a clicking from the fireplace to my right drew my eyes in that direction. A sudden spark ignited the logs in to life. At first the flames were small, but within seconds they spread over the untouched wood like a disease, growing bigger as their insatiable hunger was appeased. Justin was crouched at the side looking in to the fire.

"Mesmerising aren't they?" he said, moving over to a nearby table. He placed a large jerry can down with a dull thud. Not once did he turn to look at me. All I could see was the back of his head.

"If you say so."

"Oh, but they are. Look how they grow, bigger and stronger, the hotter they burn. So destructive and powerful. Like me."

I couldn't believe what I witnessed next. Justin reached out his hand and put it in the middle of the fire. The flames licked at his flesh, his face twisting with the agony. But still he kept it there.

"You're crazy!"

I wasn't sure whether it was the wind howling through the eves, Justin, or even the house itself, laughing at me. An insane laugh. The kind a person only hears in their nightmares.

He retracted his hand and slowly turned towards me, cradling the burnt lump. His eyes locked straight on to mine, his lips pulled back in a perverse snarl. He moved his hand up towards his mouth. His bloated tongue flickered between his teeth, licking the burnt skin.

"Mmm, it tastes good," he drooled, then pointed it towards me. "Want a taste?"

"You sick, twisted bastard."

I was struggling to hold on to my own sanity. He came towards me, trying to force his fingers down my throat. I coughed and spluttered, gagging on the taste. Vomit exploded from my mouth. I couldn't breathe. He was smothering me, laughing incessantly in my ear. I could see the enjoyment on his face.

He took his hand out of my mouth and walked towards the kitchen. I couldn't believe how much had changed in him, in such a short amount of time. He had gone from the most perfect guy I'd ever met, to the most hideous and crazy. How was it possible for someone to hide their true nature the way he had?

I wondered, trying to get my breath back. It wasn't natural. If someone else had been telling me this story, I never would've believed it. But there it was, right in front of me. My brain just couldn't understand it.

I tried to keep my breathing steady in order to conserve my energy. I would need all of it, before the night was over. I felt a new confidence growing in me. Something happens to a person when they witness so much horror. It's hard to explain. The mind switches off its inhibitions, the part that knows what it sees is wrong. It convinces itself that everything around you is normal, even though it's far from it. I don't know whether it's something to do with adrenaline, or whether everybody has a place in their psyche that they can hide away in, where no one else can find them, or get to them. It creates a sense of hope. False hope.

The cursing and banging in the kitchen told me that he might be in there for some time. I peered over the top of the sofa. He was rooting around in the cupboards and drawers at the other end of the kitchen. It seemed as though he was focused on finding something.

"Rachel," he called over his shoulder. "Do you want a sandwich?"

It took me a few seconds to understand what he'd said. My ears heard the words, but my brain didn't understand them at first. Then like a light bulb switching on, a thought struck me.

I took a breath. "Yes, please. If it's no bother."

"For you," he replied, looking over his shoulder at me. "Nothing is a bother."

I watched him as he moved over to the fridge and stuck his head inside. The power must have been out, as there was no light, or electrical humming coming from inside.

His head popped up above the fridge door. He was smiling. "Fancy chicken? I can do you a nice chicken and mayo sub. Yes, we'll have chicken."

He disappeared again in to the fridge before closing it

with his foot and walking over to the counter. I heard him whistling the Davy Crockett theme tune, as he worked. It was surreal. One minute he was putting his hand into a burning fire, the next he was making me a sandwich. If I hadn't been so terrified, I probably would've laughed at it.

He came over with the plate and handed me the sub. Bluish green mould was growing on top.

"Enjoy," he said, passing me the plate.

My hands wouldn't stop shaking, as I took it from him. "Thank you."

"You're welcome, sugar pie." He left and went back to the kitchen.

Within seconds I heard him rooting around in the kitchen again. What was he searching for? I wondered, but I didn't spend too much time thinking about it. My moment had come.

Carefully, I placed the sub on the floor, trying as hard as I could not to make a sound. I peered over the top of the sofa again. He hadn't heard anything. His back was to me. I moved my legs over the side of the sofa, so that I was sitting up. Not once did I take my eyes off the kitchen. God knows what he would do to me, I thought, if he found me?

My body protested, but I fought it off. My vision swam, as I slowly stood up. The dizzying feeling made me feel sick. Somehow I kept myself from puking. My legs were wobbly but they would do.

I tiptoed towards the door. I had to get out. This time I wouldn't run into the woods. Justin always kept his cell phone in the car, which was always unlocked. If I could get to the car and lock myself in, then I could call for help. I'd be safe. Free. I reached out my hand. The door knob was centimetres from my grasp. I held my breath, taking one last look over my shoulder. Still he was searching. I felt the door grind in my hand, as I turned the handle. My heart was racing, blood pounding in my ears.

"For fuck sake," he screamed, slamming his hand down on the counter. "I can't find it."

I shot back to the sofa, placing myself in the position I had been in. Had he seen me? Had he known I was moving? He looked at me inquisitively.

"Did you move?"

"N-n-no."

He raised a disbelieving eyebrow. "Are you sure? Liars go to hell you know."

"I-I'm not lying, I swear."

He scratched his chin. "How's the sandwich?"

"It's lovely. Thank you." I couldn't take my eyes off of him.

"Hmm, well, I'm going to be in the back room for a second."

Was he testing me? I wondered. Tempting me to try and run again.

"I won't be a minute. But when I come back, I've got lots of games for us to play. What do you think?"

"S-sounds good."

"Awesome."

I watched him leave the room. This time I didn't waste a single second, trying to guess what he was doing. Once I heard his footsteps enter the other room, I bolted.

My knee smashed against the coffee table as I ran past. Blinding pain shot up through my leg. The jerry can toppled over with a loud bang. It must have echoed through the silent house. I stopped to listen out for any footsteps heading towards the living room. Nothing. There was no time to lose. Ignoring the pain, I grabbed hold of the door and yanked it hard, not expecting it to open first time. A rush of cold wind blasted me in the face, filling my lungs with clean air. Freedom.

Just as I was about to shoot down the porch steps, heavy hands grabbed me around the waist and pulled me back in. The door slammed shut.

"You'll catch your death out there," Justin said. "We don't want that now do we?"

I kicked and screamed, trying to wriggle loose of his arms.

He was strong. He lifted me off the ground with ease and carried me towards the kitchen. The strength he possessed seemed unnatural. I wondered if he had been taking drugs, a performance enhancer, steroids, something like that. It was the only possible reason that my brain could cope with, as to why he had changed so much.

He slammed me down onto one of the wooden chairs. I'm surprised the legs didn't buckle out beneath it. I scratched at him, bit him, tried anything I could to get free. All he did was laugh it off. He knew I couldn't hurt him.

"I like it rough," he sneered, taking out a piece of rope that was tucked into the waistband of his jeans.

I spat in his face. "Let me go. I want to go home."

He wiped the spittle off his face. "This is home now. You're never going anywhere again. Like the rest of them, you'll be staying here with me."

"The rest of them? What're you talking about?"

"You'll find out soon enough, sugar pie. Now you hold still while I tie you up. We're gonna have ourselves a party."

First he bound my ankles with the coarse straw rope and then tied my hands behind my back, so that I couldn't move on the chair. The material scratched and bit into my skin, leaving red friction burns. I couldn't take anymore.

"Please," I sobbed. "Let me go, I promise I won't tell anybody. Nobody has to ever know about this. I can keep a secret. I swear I can, just let me go."

His hand came flying across my face in a wild swing. There was a loud slap followed by a burning sensation as he struck me. Blood trickled from my bottom lip. I spat out a tooth.

"Close your fucking pie hole, whore. I do hate a woman that does nothing but whine. Here I am, trying to provide you with a damn fine, entertaining evening and you throw it right back in my face. Peachy, ain't it? Just as ungrateful as all the rest. There's just no pleasing some people."

He left me sitting in the chair and walked over towards

the fireplace.

"Look at the damn mess you've made in here. There's lighter fluid all over the floor. I'm going to make you lick that up like a dog later."

He picked something up by the door. At first I wasn't sure what it was. Again he had his back to me, so that I couldn't see anything. He crouched down by the fire.

"I found my toy," he said, talking more to himself than to me. "It was out in the back room. It's funny how things are always in the last place that you look, but then again, I guess they would be. Why would a person continue looking when they've found the object? Some sayings just don't make sense. Take for example this one. A watched pot never boils. What the fuck does that mean? It just makes no damn sense. Wouldn't you agree?"

"You're crazy."

"I think we've established that already."

I tried to crane my neck to see what he was doing down by the fire. But I couldn't see. His broad shoulders blocked my view.

"Take, for example, this poker. I'm watching it and it's getting hotter. Prime example of how lame that saying is."

Poker? Why would he need a poker? I wondered.

He came back over towards me, placing a chair right in front of me and sitting himself down on it backwards. He folded his arms over the back of it and leant his chin on **them** (?).

"So, what shall we do first?"

"What do you mean?"

"Well that there poker, it's gonna take a good few minutes to heat up fully, so until then, what would you like to do?"

"I'd like to go home."

Tears coursed down my cheeks. I didn't care if he thought I was weak, or what he thought about me. The opinions of a mad man don't matter. Nothing mattered to me, except staying alive. But I wasn't even sure I was going to be capable of that. I was almost resigned to my fate.

"W-what are you going to do to me?" I asked.
"Why all the tears? Are you afraid of me?"
"Yes."

His eyes darkened over. He lowered his head, keeping his eyes fixed on mine, as he sucked in the air through his teeth. "That's sensible." He stood up. "Because you should be."

I closed my eyes, unable to bear anymore. I wanted it to end. Listening to his footsteps walk back over to the fireplace, whistling the Davy Crockett tune again, I realised what he was going to do to me. As much as I wanted everything to be over, there was no way it was going to be quick, or easy. Torture is one of the most inhumane things a person can do to another human being. It strips away their dignity, the very thing that makes them a person. Only a monster could do that. And that's what Justin had become. A monster.

He came back over to me, breathing on me. I could smell his putrid breath and burnt hand, as he got close. The inside of my eyelid had turned an orange colour. I could feel heat. My eyes slowly opened. The poker was only an inch away from them, the red hot metal making them water.

"Did you know that eyeballs explode when they're exposed to high temperatures? Now I'm thinking that's probably a myth, but I've always wanted to try it out."

"No, please," I screamed. "Justin, please don't. Do you remember, you said you liked my eyes? You said they were pretty. Wouldn't it be better to leave them?"

He stopped to think about it for a second. "Hmm, they are your best feature. I guess I'll have to have some fun elsewhere."

His hand lifted up my skirt, revealing my milky white thighs. He brought the burning metal down against them.

My body writhed in agony, as I let out a high pitched scream. The pain was excruciating. At first, red hot and then freezing cold as the nerve receptors in the skin began to fire and die. He did one thigh and then the other. The smell was like nothing else in this world. It was like a cross between burnt chicken and a slaughter house. I thought I would pass out from the pain. Eventually it goes numb. Everything goes numb. I still can't wear short skirts now.

I felt him pull the poker away.

"Nah, that's boring. How about here?"

Before I could ready myself, the sharp tip of the poker jabbed through my shoulder. I almost bit my tongue off as my jaw clenched shut. His laughter was ringing in my ears. This time I was sick. I'm surprised the chair didn't fall over, as my body was racked with spasms. He pulled the poker out. There was no blood, only a small trickle oozing from the newly punctured hole. The heat had cauterised the wound. He clearly had no plans to kill me quickly.

"This seems to have cooled down a little. I'll be back."

He left me sitting on the chair, semi-conscious. I don't recall much about what happened next. Everything's a little hazy. All I can remember is suddenly feeling the ropes slacken around my wrists. Somehow, I'd been saved. I'd been given a second chance to escape.

Ignoring the pain as much as I could, I untied my ankles. As I looked up, I could have sworn I saw the young girl from the picture in the kitchen window. I blinked to clear my eyes and the vision was gone. It must have been my imagination playing tricks on me after everything my body had been through. I blocked it from my mind and focused on my escape.

Justin was still crouched down by the fire. I crept over to the sink. He'd been stupid enough to leave out the bread board when he'd made me a sandwich. It was something I could use. I picked it up and made my way towards the living room. My eyes blazing with deadly intent. I'd make that bastard pay for everything he'd put me through. He would feel every tear by the time I was done.

Three steps.
I'll make him pay.
Two steps.
Sick fuck.
One step.

I brought the hard wooden surface of the chopping board down across the back of his head with my uninjured arm, the other burning with pain. He hit the floor with a thud, sending the red hot poker skidding away from him. A primal scream tore from my throat. Harder and harder I smashed his head with the board. My lungs were burning with the effort. Still I continued. Bits of brain matter, skull and blood sprayed through the air like a gruesome fountain.

I don't know why I stopped, but I did. My chest heaving in rapid bursts. I wiped blood from my face with the back of my hand, slinging my weapon to the floor. It landed with a crash. But there was also a splash.

The lighter fluid had spilt from the Jerry can on the floor. It was everywhere. A huge puddle of it had started to form and now it was beginning to soak in to the carpet, the furniture, everything. It was around my feet, Justin's body was laying in it, Jesus, it had even managed to stretch to the front door. I didn't realise just how much liquid one of those cans could hold. It was then I recognised my mistake.

The puddle was inching towards the poker. I ran.

The heat singed the back of my heels as the living room went up like a raging fireball. The flames followed me, stretching towards the clean air in the hallway, grabbing at anything it could feed on. I couldn't breathe, where the air had been sucked out of the house by the fire. I didn't stop moving, just ran. My only other escape was the back door.

I flung myself in to it, but bounced straight back off. I could hear the fire roaring behind me. It wasn't going to take long for it to spread.

I stood up and pulled at the door. It didn't budge, just sat there mocking me and my feeble attempt at trying to open it. I felt so weak. I wanted to collapse, but knew I couldn't. Not if I wanted to live. I pulled harder and harder, but it didn't even rattle in the frame. I was trapped.

"Rachel, oh Rachel. Come back, sugar pie."

I couldn't believe it. Justin was standing in the doorway,

wreathed in flames. It wasn't possible. He'd been in the middle of the room when it ignited. He should've been dead, burnt to a crisp. But there he was, his dark eyes stared at me with murderous intent.

"You're not going anywhere. I've told you a thousand times already, no one ever leaves this house. Even if you get away, I'll follow you. You'll never be rid of me, Rachel. You may as well give in."

"Screw you."

He lurched down the corridor, howling, bouncing from wall to wall, as he spread the fire deeper in to the house. He lunged at me with his burning hands, but I managed to dodge, shooting up the stairs, my only escape route blocked off. There was nowhere left to run except up. Thinking about it now, it probably wasn't my best move.

I felt a tugging at my ankles. Justin had grabbed hold of my foot through the stair rail. The fire was crawling up his arm. I must have had lighter fluid on my shoe because it burst in to flames. I kicked it in to his face and scrambled up the rest of the stairs.

I wasn't thinking straight. Where the hell could I run to up here, I thought. I felt like a rat caught in a trap.

"I'm coming to get you."

I peered over the banister.

"Peek-a-boo."

He grabbed me and began to close his hands around my throat. The heat was unbearable. I could feel it licking at my skin, wanting to consume me. I was going to pass out. I could feel it, the edges of my vision starting to go black. I had to do something. Fast.

Out of the corner of my eye, I glimpsed an old rocking chair. I could feel his grip tightening. I stretched for the chair. Any second and I'd be dead. My fingertips scratched at it. I pushed him backwards trying to give myself some room. I reached it with one hand. It slipped from my fingers. Everything was going dark, but I gave one final lunge.

The chair swung in an arc towards his head, bringing it down as hard as I could. Again and again I hit him. Still he struggled. I gave it one more try.

The chair shattered across his shoulders, knocking him unconscious. At least that's what I hoped. Hot air filled my lungs as I took deep breaths. Acrid smoke was beginning to climb its way up through the floorboards. I ran in to the child's bedroom and shut the door, trying to block out the smoke. I used everything I could think of. The wardrobe, rotten bed sheets, even my own hoodie. But still it seeped through.

Shutters banged. Outside it sounded as if the birds were going crazy, beating their wings against the house. No doubt they were scared by the fire. So was I.

Justin's words echoed through me.

You'll never be rid of me, Rachel. You may as well give in.

I was trapped...

CHAPTER TWENTY

"Is that it?" David asked, his eyes narrowing. "Surely that can't be all?"

"That's it," Rachel replied. She was getting tired of his constant questioning. "The flames got out of control and then the fire department arrived, the end."

"But how did you escape? What happened to Justin?"

"For Christ sake, David, there isn't any more to tell. He died, the house burnt down. I thought you were going to try and help me get through this. Instead, all you've done is dredge up all these memories. Don't you understand how hard it is for me?"

"Of course I understand, I just want to help you."

People were beginning to look now, their nervous faces sticking out like ghosts in the gloom, wondering if the sudden uproar would spill over on to their tables. But she didn't care.

"That's the thing though, you don't understand. No one has ever understood what I've had to go through." Her blood was boiling now. She could feel the surge of anger coursing through her veins. She wanted to stop but she couldn't. "You weren't there, how could you understand? I've lived the same nightmare again and again for three years. I can't sleep, I can't go out alone. Jesus, I can't even come back to visit my parents because it's too hard to remember. That one night has taken away my life. My only comfort was knowing that the house no longer stood. But now it's back and it will never be over. I just want it to be over."

They sat there in silence, Rachel sobbing into her napkin. A blonde waiter came over to ask if everything was okay; some of the other customers were apparently complaining about her outburst. Well screw them, she thought. The whole damn world could go to hell for all she cared. David informed the waiter that everything was fine, but could they have the cheque. The guy shot off in the direction of the bar.

Embarrassment had started to seep in; Rachel couldn't believe that she had gone through that entire tirade in the middle of a restaurant. She could feel her cheeks burning, as they turned scarlet in colour. She heard David fidget in his seat. No doubt he was as embarrassed as she was. Everything she touched just went wrong.

"Look, I'm sorry if I pushed you too hard." David said, breaking the silence. "I'm used to patients that are tough to crack."

"Forget it," Rachel replied. "I just feel so trapped, David. I don't know what to do anymore. I'm so angry all the time."

"It's okay."

"It's not your fault. This was my idea. I thought it would help to talk to someone, but I guess I was wrong."

"I wouldn't say that. It's hard to confront our greatest fears and I think just by getting this far, you've taken a huge step in dealing with it."

She paused for a moment, not sure what to say.

"And you've certainly made a new friend," he added, with a smile.

"Thank you."

"Anytime. Although, maybe next time we could just go out for a meal. No talk of houses."

Rachel felt that familiar sense of relief that she had only ever experienced with the man sitting opposite her.

"I'd love to see you again, but I don't know when I will be leaving town." The sooner the better, she thought. "Maybe you could drive up to Fort Kent for a visit?"

"That would be great. I've got some vacation time due next month. I'll come up then."

"Excellent."

Her heart soared. It hadn't been an easy night, but maybe

it was worth fighting through the pain of her memories after all. Maybe this was the turning point? Life certainly couldn't get any worse, she thought.

The waiter returned with the cheque. Rachel wanted to pay her half, but David refused to take any money.

"How are you getting home?" he asked.

"Ummm, I was going to call a cab to take me to the bed and breakfast."

"I can't let you do that. How about I drop you off?"

"I couldn't ask you to do that. You've got your new place to sort out."

"You're not asking, I'm offering." He smiled at her. "Honest it's no trouble."

"Well, if you're sure?"

"I wouldn't have asked if I wasn't. I'll just go and pay the bill."

Rachel waited by the front door of the restaurant. A sudden flash of light, followed by a low rumble, announced the storm was picking up again. She was glad David had offered to drive her back. The rain was coming down so hard it looked like a waterfall coming from the sky. There was no way she wanted to wait for a cab out in that. She heard footsteps behind her.

"Shall we get going?" he asked, offering her his arm.

She took it, and the two of them walked out into the stormy night.

The rain pelted against them as they shot across the car park towards the car. David tried to shield them with his jacket, but the wind was blowing so hard, the rain was lashing down sideways. As they reached the car, he swung the passenger door open and Rachel jumped in. Within seconds he joined her, shutting the rain out behind him.

"Wow, this storm is wild," he said, shaking the loose drops out of his hair.

"I know. I've never known a storm like this before. I hope Nathan and Becky are okay."

"I'm sure they're fine."

It went quiet in the confined space of the vehicle, as Rachel buckled her seatbelt. She still felt guilty for blowing her top in the restaurant. There was one thing that had been bugging her all night.

"What is it with you and Nathan? He really seems to have a problem with you."

"I don't know. You'll have to ask him."

She sat back and stared out of the window. "There must be a reason. Come on, tell me. I told you all of my secrets."

David stopped fiddling with his seat and looked at her. "I can't. Sorry."

Rachel was disappointed and a little annoyed. "You don't trust me."

"It's not that, it's-"

"Then tell me."

David sighed, gripping the steering wheel tight. "Okay, but you'll have to promise me you won't say anything."

"I won't."

"Promise?"

"Yeah okay, I promise."

He fidgeted in his seat and adjusted the rear view mirror. "Nathan was one of my first patients."

"Oh my God, why? What was wrong with him?"

"There was a huge shoot out over on route fifty. He saw several good men get shot and die that day. He was sent to me with P.T.S.D."

"What's that?"

"It's post-traumatic stress disorder. A lot of soldiers, or people in any stressful situations, can suffer from it."

Rachel was shocked. Nathan was one of her best friends and had been since they were children. She hated to think of him suffering. It did explain a lot about his behaviour though, she thought. It was another thing that she had to feel guilty for. Maybe if she had been here, then she could have helped him through it. It seemed as though she wasn't the only person that had changed since she left.

"Anyway," David continued. "When he came to me he was showing extreme signs. Bouts of violence and uncontrollable anger, insomnia and anxiety were all present. There were complaints about his drinking. I tried to help him as best I could, but…" he let the sentence trail off. He cleared his throat. "It's getting late, but is it too late for a coffee?"

"Erm." She was taken aback by the sudden change of subject. "I don't think there will be anywhere open at this time of night."

"You could come back to my new place. It might be nice to have some company, as it's my first night there."

Was there a hint of something else in his voice? She wondered. In a way she hoped there was, but she wasn't ready for anything like that yet. Although she doubted Becky would be home very early. She didn't want to be alone with only the ghosts of her past to keep her occupied.

"Just coffee." It was more of a statement than a question.

"Of course."

"Okay then, that would be lovely."

As she got herself comfy in the passenger seat, David turned the key in the ignition. The engine hummed to life, and the wheels drifted forward across the car park towards the main road.

Rachel's mind was racing with jumbled thoughts of the past. And Nathan. David had been a perfect gentleman all evening and she felt bad that she hadn't been as honest with him, as he had been with her. Nathan was in a mess, by all accounts, and she didn't want to end up in the same predicament.

"Do you think I have P.T.S.D.?" she asked, not taking her eyes off the open fields speeding past in the window.

"It's a possibility. You certainly went through a traumatic experience. From what you've told me, you've been exhibiting some of the text book symptoms."

The car filled with silence again. Oppressive. It was as if there was something growing in between them.

"I wasn't being completely honest with you earlier."

"Oh?"

Rachel took a deep breath. "There's a bit more to the story than I told you."

David kept his eyes firmly on the road. "Go on."

"I'm not sure I can." Her heart was beginning to race, the beat matching the tapping of the windscreen wipers swishing backwards and forwards to clear the rain. "It's never really been clear to me, as if I've shut it away."

"Maybe if you closed your eyes, it would help."

"I don't know."

"Try it. You're safe here."

It was time she let go. She closed her eyes.

"The fire was everywhere. The thick smoke filled my lungs, making me choke. I knew if I didn't get out, I would die…"

***

It was as if the house was trying to join the fight. The flames licked at my flesh, searing the skin. Beams began to crack and splinter. But they held. I didn't know how long it would be before they started falling. I ran straight to the window in the upstairs bedroom. It was getting darker in the confined space. I couldn't see anything. My eyes were streaming with tears, a mixture of sweat and acrid smoke. I had no idea where Justin was. As far as I knew, he was still sprawled out on the landing where I left him.

As I reached the window, my only thought was to try and jump; I knew at that kind of height, my legs would probably break, but broken bones could be mended. Death is forever.

I unhooked the latch and went to push the glass upwards. It didn't budge, not even an inch. I tried again. Still nothing. Panic started to seep in, as the fire licked at my heels. Years of dirt and grime had jammed it shut. I was trapped. The only other way out of the house was to go downstairs and back out the window I had broken earlier, but the fire was worse down there. The living room no longer existed and the kitchen was slowly being consumed. The whole house was made of wood. It wouldn't take long for the rest to go up in flames.

I tried to stem the panic rising in me by taking deep breaths, but I couldn't breathe. The smoke was too thick. My knees buckled beneath me and I fell to the floor, my head banging on the wood. The blow didn't knock me out, but I wish it had. I can't really explain what happened next. All I remember is the horror.

At first I thought I had passed out, drifting through some hellish nightmare of my own creation. Coming towards me, their arms outstretched, were the dolls. I watched them as some dragged their hideous bodies closer, their fingers scratching along the floor. It was the most terrifying thing I'd ever seen in my life. I still see them now, on nights when it's cold and dark. I see them in the shadows and in my dreams when I sleep. I don't think I'll ever forget them.

Scratching to my right made my ears prick up. I turned my head. Standing right beside me was the one with its face half smashed in, the fire reflecting off its single eye. In its hand the knife hung over my head, poised to end my life.

I rolled away from the blade, as it slashed down towards my face. The red hot sting of the edge biting into my cheek, as the full force of it missed. I tried to scramble to my feet, but I lost my footing. My back slammed into the dresser with a loud crash. The doll came straight for me, lunging for my throat. Shooting my legs out like pistons, I sent it howling across the room. Within seconds the others were on me, their grisly fingers scratching and pulling at me.

I fought for my life in that bedroom. They were like the Devil's rejects spat from hell. The shrieking rose louder as they attacked. If the fire didn't get me, the dolls would.

My legs and arms seemed to work on their own, kicking and punching out at my attackers. Their limbs snapped and twisted, but still they came at me. One by one I fought them down, smashing their hideous bodies to pieces. Then the leader was back. It snarled at me. The knife glinted in the flames.

"You fucking slut, you're not going anywhere."

Something in me snapped. I don't know how and I don't

know if it was my imagination, but there was something in the voice, something familiar. For a split second, it sounded like Justin. Whatever it was, it turned my heart to stone.

"Come and get me, bitch."

We flew at each other like wraiths. The doll slashed at me with the knife, but I swung my leg as hard as I could. It dodged my kick and came at me harder. I grabbed the deformed body, dashing it against the wall. I'll never forget the screaming. It tore through my soul to my very core. And then it was silent, only the roaring of the flames could be heard. The blade sat lifeless on the floor. I ran.

The hallway was engulfed in flames, as the house was beginning to collapse in on itself. There was no way out. The stairs had gone, eaten away by the all-consuming flames.

I felt something grab at my ankle. My instincts caused me to kick out, thinking it was the doll back for revenge.

"Rachel, please help me."

I couldn't move. Justin had a hold of my leg, clawing at me. I don't know whether it was insanity or fear in his eyes.

"Please, I love you."

"Screw you."

I kicked him in the head, knocking him unconscious. He had fooled us all. I wasn't about to let him do it to me twice. I knew that within minutes, the building would crumple like a house of cards. Then I saw it. The window at the end of the hallway.

Taking a deep breath, I prayed my idea would work. I covered my face with my arms and charged forward. Straight at the window...

***

Nathan took a long drag on his cigarette before tossing it to the floor. He couldn't believe the weather, so uncharacteristically stormy for the time of year. He could feel the electricity in the air. It made the hairs on his neck stand on edge. It was as if something was building, an ominous portent. He only hoped it was his imagination.

High heeled footsteps behind him drew his attention.

"Hey, I wondered where you got to," Becky said, her blonde hair billowing out behind her in the wind. "Are you coming back inside? It's getting wild out here."

"Yeah I guess we should be going back in. We don't want you catching pneumonia."

She smiled, a cheeky twinkle in her eyes. "Well I'm sure you could nurse me back to health."

He grabbed her around the waist, pulling her in close to him. The rain tapped on the tin roof of the shelter. "Could I now?"

Before she could answer, their lips locked together. His tongue explored the velvet softness of her mouth. It felt good. All his doubts and fears evaporated in that moment. Everything would be fine, he thought. Maybe it was possible to get his life back on track, to forget the past and move forward.

They parted, Becky's face a slight pink.

"Wow," she said, breathless.

"Good?"

"Definitely good."

They both laughed. Something coming along the road caught Nathan's attention. He stepped forward from under the tin cover.

"What is it, Nate?"

He didn't answer, just stared at the speeding car. His fear rose like bile in his throat.

"Talk to me, Nathan. What's wrong?"

He spun towards her and grabbed her roughly by the shoulders. "Did Rachel take her car on the date?"

"I-I don't-"

"Did she or didn't she?"

"Ow, Nathan you're hurting me."

"TELL ME!"

"No I don't think she did. David was driving. What the hell is wrong with you?"

He let go of her and stalked off towards his own car.

Becky followed him in to the rain. She grabbed him by the wrist.

"What's wrong? Why do you need to know?"

"We've got to get to the sheriff's office," Nathan replied, his words strained. "He's taking her to the house."

"Why? Why would he take her to the house?"

"He owns it. He isn't interested in helping her."

"But why? What are you talking about?"

Nathan's fear was growing. He had to hurry.

"Don't you see," he said. "He wants to recreate the past." His eyes looked towards the house. The final piece of the puzzle slotted into place. "He's Justin's brother."

***

"It felt like I was falling forever," Rachel said. Her eyes were still shut tight, picturing the memories. She sounded as though she was in some kind of trance. "When I finally hit the ground, my mind was blank. The fall sprained my ankle, but thankfully the bones were still intact. Behind me I could hear the beams of the house falling. To me it sounded as if it was screaming, but that was more likely my imagination. It was over. Justin was dead. Somehow, I'd survived."

She took a deep breath as she finished. The engine of the Prius hummed through the car. She could feel it was moving along at a speed, but she didn't open her eyes. Something in her had changed. It was as if the shackles of her past had been taken off of her. She hadn't felt this way since before that night.

"So, you left Justin in there to die?" David asked.

The heat in the car was making Rachel feel drowsy. "After what he had done, I wasn't about to save him."

"Don't you think it was up to the law to decide what happened to him? Do you not feel guilty?"

The locket around her neck suddenly burned, it felt heavy.

"I didn't want to be there. I didn't ask him to murder my friends. I didn't ask him to try and kill me."

David said nothing. They sat in silence. Then Rachel

heard a familiar sound. Gravel crunching beneath the tyres, as the car ground to a halt. Terror gripped her like a rope around her throat.

Her eyes opened.

She wanted to scream, but nothing would come.

There was the house in front of the car, its white washed wooden panels, standing out clear in the black sky. The black lifeless windows looking out over the countryside. It was exactly the same as she remembered it in her dreams.

"Don't be frightened, Rachel," David said, reaching out towards her.

"Why have you brought me here?" she growled. "You sick bastard."

She swung the car door open and jumped out.

"Rachel, come back." He followed her out of the car. "It's not-"

The sentence was cut short. She wasn't there. He spun around, searching for her. But she was nowhere to be seen.

"Rachel, please come back. We can talk. You need to confront your fears. This'll be good for-"

He never finished the sentence. His body was out cold before he hit the floor. A puddle of blood was beginning to form on the gravel driveway.

Rachel stood over him, a sharp stone in her hand. Spittle hung from one corner of her mouth. Her eyes were wild. Blackbirds were beginning to gather on the roof of the porch. Lightning flashed.

"Rachel's not here right now. Can I take a message?"

CHAPTER TWENTY-ONE

"Rachel," David said, his face smeared with his own blood. "If you just let me go, we can work this out."

"Nope. I can't do that, sugar pie. If I let you go, you'll run away and we don't want that."

He couldn't believe this was happening to him. Only a short while ago he was having a pleasant meal with a kind, but troubled young girl. It had been stupid to agree to this. When he met her, he had sensed that she may be deeply disturbed, but he hadn't seen her as a textbook schizophrenic. A part of him still wasn't convinced she was. There was something not right.

"You can't keep me locked up, Rachel. You know that."

"This is my land, I can do what the fuck I like."

Her land? David thought. Surely she didn't think that she owned this house.

"This is my house now. My father owns the place. Mr Langrishe."

She lunged at him with the knife, placing it firmly against his throat. Her tongue whipped back and forth along her bottom lip. Her eyes were wild. "How dare you speak to me in that manner? I made this place what it is. No one is going to take it away from me. All these loved up teenagers come strolling in here thinking they can turn it into a house of ill repute. Well I showed them what love is. Love is coming home and seeing your wife dead, her body hanging from the ceiling like a piñata at a child's party. She was my world. Then she was gone. We were meant to be together forever. Me and my sugar pie. We'll damn you. Damn every one of you."

She pulled the knife away. A thin trickle of blood ran down beneath David's shirt collar. His mind raced. Three years ago when this happened, the official reports claimed Rachel had insisted Justin went insane all of a sudden, spouting similar statements. He had also used the term 'sugar pie' it claimed. Now it seemed as though Rachel was experiencing the same demented thoughts. It was impossible for two people to have the same psychosis. Wasn't it? Never in all his life had he heard of two separate events taking the same, twisted turns.

He watched her, as she sat down on the edge of the table. The knife turned in her hand. She didn't once take her eyes off of it.

Being a professional psychologist, the supernatural had always been something to sneer at. Pure hokum. But now, David wondered if it was all true. There was certainly something amiss. Something that wasn't psychological. It was in her eyes, her manner, her speech. It was everything about her. She had changed almost completely since the beginning of the evening. But how, he wondered. Had she been possessed? With his current predicament, he realised it may be fatal to rule out any possibility.

The room had started to grow cold, despite the fire, which was beginning to die. The old house seemed to be settling for the long night ahead. The torrential rain lashed against the windows, the tapping rising and falling with the wind. Without moving his head, he looked around the kitchen. There were only two ways out: through a window, or the door. With his wrists and ankles bound to the chair, there was no escape. For a split second, he could have sworn there was somebody standing outside the window. He blinked. There was nothing there. Nobody knew they were up here. The smell of burnt flesh drifted up to his nostrils, as pain seared across his chest. Tears mingled with the blood on his cheeks. He silently prayed to God that it would be over soon. That the end would be quick.

"Are you going to kill me, Hiram? It is Hiram I'm speaking

to, isn't it?"

Rachel's face looked puzzled. "Oh no, my love. And yes I'm going to gut you like a fish. How can we be together if I don't?"

If not Hiram, David thought, then who? "Tell me something, do you remember my brother?"

There was silence for a moment. It was as if the words had hit a chord in her.

"His name was Justin," David added.

"So many kids come through here. He could've been any one of the dirty pigs."

"Who are you?"

Rachel sneered. "Haven't you worked it out yet?" She stood up, her arms stretching outwards. "Don't you see? I'm all of them. Every damn one. I'm the windows, doors, every brick and floorboard. I'm the house of wood."

David shook his head. "N-N-No, that's not possible. How can that be?"

"Hiram was stupid to build here. He wasn't the first. I've been here longer than people realise. Oh yes, I sent him mad. It wasn't hard. Booze is the perfect thing to send a man crazy. Crazy enough to kill his own family."

"It's not possible. Houses aren't alive. How is it possible? How can you possess people?"

"Aren't we a curious little one? Curiosity killed the cat, you know. It's what got those brats up there killed." Rachel strolled over to the kitchen window. "If enough bad is committed in one place, it leaves a mark. Like cancer, it eats through the very soul of a place. A clever boy like you must know that."

"You're evil."

Again, Rachel flew at him. This time the chair bowled over backwards with the two of them. David's head smashed down hard on the wooden floor. Bright sparks covered his vision. She was so close, he could smell her on top of him.

"You fucking son of a bitch," she spat in to his face. Thunder roared outside. "How dare you judge me? You don't know what it's like. Time and time again they come, but still they don't leave me alone. So, I thought I would have some fun. Jacob thought his father had killed his mother. When he saw her dead body lying on the bed, he thought Hiram could've done that. He was a sentimental sap. Jacob went for him like a wild beast. The knife was in Hiram's hand. It just came up before he realised. The blood. The blood was everywhere. I enjoyed toying with them. Their souls are still here. I've collected so many more since then. The more people fear me, the stronger I get. And now…"

There was a glint in the eyes. Her lips were drawn back into a snarl, spittle dripped down onto David's forehead.

"You're going to be our newest member."

A piercing scream filled the night air, integrating with the sound of thunder. The deadly blade made a sucking sound, as it was extracted from between his ribs. David could've sworn there was someone else in the room, as the edges of his vision closed in on him.

***

"But Pa, I know there's something going on up there. You've got to believe me." Nathan was practically screaming the words. He was beginning to wish that he hadn't drunk anything tonight. His eyes kept blurring in and out of focus. "Just give me a handful of guys to go and check it out."

"I can't do that, Nate. Not on a hunch." Sheriff Ross sat back in his brown, wood and leather office chair. He brought his hands together under his chin. He looked bored, as though he would rather be anywhere else than in his office late at night. "I'm sorry. I can't do it."

Nathan was pacing around the room. He slammed his fist down hard on the desk. "You have to do something. Rachel could be in danger."

"The James girl? Trouble seems to follow her like a lost puppy wherever she goes." The sheriff leant forward. "But that don't change a thing. If you wanna go charging out there like some lunatic at this hour, then that's your business."

"But Pa, you know what happened last time. I came to you and you did nothing until it was too late. Can't you see, it's happening again."

"Sorry Nathan, but I think you should leave. Now."

"But -"

"Nathan!"

"Fine."

It was useless to argue. He spun around to leave, the white fluorescent light blinding him as he turned.

"Nate, if I were you I'd stay away. You've wasted enough damn time, pining after her. Trust me son, no woman is worth it."

Nathan stopped, his head low. "I've got to help her."

"But why? She'll never look at you the way you want her to. You're a dreamer wasting your time. Just like your mother."

Fury filled Nathan's eyes, as he turned on his father, grabbing him by the collar and hoisting him off his seat.

"Don't you dare talk about Ma. Not ever."

"Calm down, son. I never meant anything by it."

Sheriff Ross slumped back in his chair, as his son dropped him and turned to leave. He adjusted his shirt.

"One more thing, deputy." He opened his drawer. "I'm going to need your badge and gun."

"What? You can't -"

"Now I know what you are going to say, Nate. But I've turned too many a blind eye for you. Your drinking's out of hand. I can't have a drunk deputy on my team. It's just the way it is, son."

Nathan couldn't believe it. His fists clenched and unclenched by his side. He wanted to punch the old son of a bitch in the mouth. How dare he call me a drunk? Nathan fumed. Not when he knew damn well there was a bottle of whiskey almost empty in the other drawer.

He reluctantly unstrapped his gun and took off his badge, slamming them down on the table. "Fuck you." He went to walk out the door.

"And the keys to the squad car. You can't be driving in your condition."

Nathan threw the keys at his father before turning to open the door. He stopped halfway through. "For your sake I hope she's okay."

***

The door of the house blasted open, just as David was about to pass out. The breath in his lungs froze, as the air turned icy cold. The pain in his side was excruciating. It felt as though his insides were going to fall out. He could feel the blood oozing out of him. His hands were crushed behind him, trapped beneath the back of the chair and the hard wooden floor.

Above him, Rachel stopped.

Something else was in the room. Watching them. Waiting.

A cawing filled the kitchen. Was death coming for him? David wondered. He turned his head to the side. He blinked his eyes, not believing what he was seeing. A blackbird sat perched on the dining table.

Rachel stood up and turned to the bird.

"Hello my little princess. Have you come to help?"

The flames in the fireplace burst into life, stretching outwards towards the furniture in the room. David thought he had died and gone to hell. The searing heat filled his lungs, as the air around him was sapped into the fire. He began to choke.

The feathers on the blackbird began to fall onto the floor, as it grew to an abnormal size. Its skull started to stretch; the black eyes growing bigger. He couldn't make out what the bird was doing. He wanted to scream. Arms began to sprout out of the body and the talons on its feet turned into toes. Small tufts of black hair began to sprout from the white skull. David closed his eyes, then opened them.

A young girl was standing by the table. Her eyes blank. Her face expressionless.

"What are you doing?" the girl asked, looking down at David.

He couldn't move. Not just because he was tied to a chair, but because he was petrified. The soulless eyes looked through him. Into him. He vomited. His mind couldn't take much more before it would crack.

"I'm getting you a new friend, Lilly," Rachel replied, sneering. "Now you go out and play on your swing."

"No."

"Go on, I've got work to do, Princess."

"I won't go," Lilly screamed.

"Don't you speak to me like that, you little shit."

The flames in the fireplace flared again. The shutters on the windows had begun to slam and bang uncontrollably. Cutlery flew around the room like a swarm of wasps. Tables and chairs had begun to splinter, sending sharp needles flying through the air. The flames in the fireplace grew to an unnatural size, sucking the air from the room. The house was getting angry.

"I won't let you hurt that girl anymore," Lilly said.

"You were my favourite. But you're like the rest of them. Now I'm going to-"

Rachel's body was flung across the room before she had finished her sentence. She smashed into the cupboards, then slumped to the floor. Lilly was on top of her in an instant.

"You've been a naughty house," Lilly smiled. "Now it's my turn to play."

Her hand disappeared inside Rachel's chest. Piercing screams erupted from her, as the small girl rooted around inside.

David didn't know what to do. Time had stopped. Any moment now it had to be over. He kept repeating it over and over in his head. He couldn't take any more. The screams became louder and louder. He could hear them mix with the small girl's laughter. Had his brother gone through the same horror? He wondered. No, deep down he knew his brother hadn't felt a thing. Justin had been the one possessed. But Rachel. His heart went out to her. She had been through this twice. If only there was something he could do.

Then it occurred to him.

The new gas pipes hadn't been properly finished. The mains pipe ran straight through the living room.

The same room that was now in chaos.

**

"How the hell are we going to get there?" Becky asked, following close behind the deputy, as they walked across the almost empty parking lot. She yanked on his arm. "Nathan, will you just stop and tell me what's going on."

He spun on his heels. "All I know is we've got to get to the house. I just know he was taking her there. Why else would they have driven past in that direction?"

"But why? Why would he want to take her up there? I don't understand."

"He owns it. This was his plan all along. To recreate what his brother did in the past. Don't you see? He's going to kill her."

"His brother?" Her mouth slowly dropped. Her eyes widened in horror. "Oh my God."

Nathan pretty much dragged her the rest of the way across the parking lot. He stopped beside a clapped out old Volvo.

"Is this your car?"

"Nope, it's the Sheriff's."

Nathan bent his arm at a forty-five degree angle, turning the elbow in to a point. Becky yelped. The driver's window smashed into a thousand tiny fragments.

"What the hell are you doing? We need to leave this to the police."

"Fuck the police. They couldn't give a damn when it happened before and they're not going to now." He got in the car, his head disappearing under the dashboard.

Within seconds, the engine choked into life.

Becky stood there, tears forming in her eyes. "What if we're too late?"

Nathan quietly prayed to God that he wouldn't be too

late. He had to get there.

"Sweet Jesus," Becky said, her eyes growing wide with fear.

Tiny tendrils of grey smoke had begun to float into the air above the hilltop. A cloud of blackbirds circled.

It was coming from the house.

***

The heat from the house was intense. Rachel thought David had the heating up too high in the car. Her eyes flickered before opening. The full horror didn't hit her straight away. Her mind took a few seconds to register. She wasn't in the car. She was in hell.

The house raged all around her. Black smoke seeped into her lungs, as she tried to stand. Her legs were pinned beneath her. She moved her head slightly to get a better look. Lying on the other side of the kitchen was David. He wasn't moving. Oh my God, she thought, please don't let him be dead. What had she done? One minute she had been in the car, finally reaching the end of her story. And then…Nothing. It was as if she had slipped into a void. Being possessed was like being stuck behind a sheet of Perspex; she could see everything going on, but couldn't stop it.

Footsteps to her left grabbed her attention. She tried to scream, but nothing would come. The ghost of Hiram grabbed her by the scruff of the neck and yanked her free. Her shoulder sprung from its socket with the force.

"Think you could get rid of me that easily, you little slut," Hiram spat at her. "I can be any of them, whenever I choose."

Rachel just stared in horror, unable to say anything.

"Oh yeah, maybe this one would look more familiar."

He slung her through the air, her body flying through the flames. She screamed, as fragments of the house bit in to her flesh; shards of glass, wooden splinters, anything the house could use for its deadly purpose. As her body hit the floor, she rolled as quickly as she could, away from the danger. She had to get out, or he would kill her. But what about David?

She looked back over at the embodiment of the house. Its features bucked and twisted, its hands covering the face. The long grey hair slowly shrunk, turning to brown. The hunched shoulders broadened out. The skin became taut and firm. It stopped. Everything stopped. He looked up. Familiar brown eyes stared back at her.

"You let him kill me."

"I didn't, Tim."

Rachel closed her eyes. It wasn't possible. She squinted as hard as she could, hoping he would go away.

"You were supposed to be my best friend," a familiar voice said.

Rachel's eyes snapped open. She was staring in to the bloodied face of Chelsea.

"How could you let him do it to me?"

"Chelsea, please, I couldn't stop him. There was nothing I could do."

A macabre grin stretched across her face. "Well, baby girl, it's your turn now."

The body bucked and twisted out of shape, Chelsea's flowing red hair dropping to the floor in clumps. Rachel couldn't take it. Her hands covered her eyes.

"No more, no more, no more."

"Hello, Rachel, did you miss me?"

Rachel's hands slowly dropped, as she backed away from the figure, sliding along the floor. "No, no you can't be, I saw you die. You died in the fire."

"Like I told you," Justin said. "I can be any of them."

Loud screams filled the night air, as the fear inside Rachel took hold. The fireplace blazed, as the house roared in triumph. There was no way out, she realised, closing her eyes. The house was finally going to get its wish. They were going to die.

CHAPTER TWENTY-TWO

The house had taken on a life of its own. The orange flames in the fireplace had shrunk. The furniture now still. It wasn't real. It seemed as if the house was waiting for something, taking a deep breath before its final onslaught. The calm before the storm.

Rachel lay prone in the corner, her face contorted with the terror coursing through her veins. This couldn't be happening, her mind screamed, not again. The pain in her battered body was almost paralysing. She tried to push herself up. The agony flooded her system, causing her vision to blur as if she was underwater. Gentle groans emanated from the kitchen. She realised David was still alive. She gritted her teeth. No one else would die for her.

A muddy boot pressed down on her broken shoulder. She screamed, tears burning her eyes.

"You're pathetic," Justin said, his voice unnaturally low. "This time you won't get away."

He picked up her limp body. Her eyelids flickered, as he carried her to the sofa. A deep groan came from her, as she was thrown on to the plastic covered surface. In a semi-unconscious state, she was dimly aware of a raucous noise outside. It sounded like some beast hitting the house.

Justin licked his lips, noticing Rachel's growing fear. She gasped. His eyes were no longer blue. The subtle light in the room bounced off the now onyx surface.

"Can you hear them?" he asked.

"W-what is it?"

"It's my children, come to play." His eyes pierced deep inside her. "They want you to say hello."

He sprung towards her, pulling her towards the window.

"No, no. Get off me you sick freak."

He smashed her head against the glass. A single crack crawled down the pane, her blood running alongside it. She remembered the dolls upstairs, their faces cracked and broken.

"Open your eyes, sugar pie."

"No."

"Open your fucking eyes."

"I won't do it."

He smashed her head again. "OPEN THEM!"

Slowly, she gave in. Blood mixed with the tears giving everything a red tint. Then she saw. Blackbirds, hundreds of them, circling overhead, their caws like macabre cries of joy.

"They'll eat your bones, sugar pie," Justin said. "I owe you."

The next thing Rachel knew, she was being dragged out of the house by her hair. Towards her death.

***

Please don't be dead. Please don't be dead. Please don't be dead.

The words were like a mantra rolling around Nathan's brain. It matched the rhythm of the windshield wipers, which could barely keep up with the downpour. He couldn't see a thing, except a black smudge on the skyline in the distance. It stood out in stark contrast to the grey clouds above. His heart was racing. All he wanted was to get to the house. But part of him wanted to turn back; to run away from his worst nightmare, instead of heading straight for it.

Lightning overhead illuminated his path. He was almost there. If only she could hang on for a few more seconds. The trees would thin out any minute and he would be there.

As the car reached the crest of the smaller hill, the full extent of the situation hit home. It was like nothing he had seen before. The blackbirds swarmed around the house like sick blowflies. Unnatural. Unholy.

For the first time in three years, he covered himself with the sign of the cross.

From out of the nearby trees, black shapes darted towards the car. The birds' bodies smashed in to the vehicle, the sheer number of them almost ramming him off the road. The car swerved left and right. The windows smashed, allowing vicious beaks to poke through. Blood, guts and feathers covered the car. Nathan was struggling to keep control. There was only one thing left to do.

He swung the car door open. The birds ripped at his skin, taking huge strips of flesh with them. He aimed the car. Then floored it.

***

Rachel sat at the base of the tree outside the house. The swing didn't move. She didn't see the explosion just below the hill. But she heard it. Her last hope of surviving. Gone. She heard the maniacal laugh coming towards her, but she didn't look towards him. She just stared at the black, lifeless windows.

"I'm afraid your friend won't be joining us this evening."

Justin's sick laughter almost deafened her, as he lifted her against the dead tree. His putrid breath filled her nostrils, his bloated tongue running the length of her neck. She felt sick.

"Mmmm, maybe I'll have some fun before I give you to my children," Justin sneered, his hand exploring under her top. "Then your soul will join them."

Rachel's eyes burned with hatred. "I stopped you before."

"You poor misguided creature. I could feel Justin screaming inside me as I tortured you. He loved you and you burnt him alive thinking he was evil. Now he's urging me on like the rest of them." He slid the knife up her arm. "They all succumb in the end."

Something in her snapped. Rachel's eyes looked straight at the abomination leering over her. She was getting angry now. "You've taken half my life away. You sick, evil bastard."

Justin laughed at her. "What're you going to do, bitch? Kill me?"

Rachel's own sadistic smile crawled across her face. "The living can't kill the dead," she said, her voice deep, more like a growl. "But I'm not so sure about the dead having a go."

Lilly had been standing behind the tree the whole time, listening. She launched herself straight at him.

The two of them flew backwards. This was her chance, Rachel realised. She sprang into action.

Sprinting towards the door, she ignored the two fighting on the floor. It was wide open. She had to get David out. He must have lost a lot of blood by now, she thought. Maybe too much? She didn't know how much blood a person could lose before it was too late. She moved faster.

The house had the last laugh. An unseen force slammed the front door shut. She tugged and slammed herself against it. Nothing budged. She was locked out.

A hand yanked her around. Half of Justin's face had been caved in. Shards of his skull protruded through the skin. His single eye leered at her.

"Did you really think that little bitch could stop me?"

**

David didn't know how much time had passed. All he could hear were agonising screams. He kept blinking in and out of consciousness. His body felt cold, despite the heat coming from the fireplace. It didn't matter anymore. He wouldn't want to live after tonight.

He started to lift up and opened his eyes.

"Get away from me," he choked. "Get away."

Lilly pointed a finger at him. He felt the ropes behind him loosen. He blinked.

"W-w-what? I-I don't understand."

"The house won't let me see my Mommy."

He shook his head, even more confused.

She looked at the blood seeping out between his fingers, then towards the exposed gas pipes.

Their eyes locked. David finally understood.

***

"You dumb bitch," Justin spat. "When're you going to learn, you can't kill me. Evil permeates this place. It will *always* survive."

Rachel had lost her burst of courage. There was nothing left to do, but die and be done with it. She had waited for the end to come countless times in the last few years. Now it was here. Let the endless silence take me, she thought. No more suffering.

Justin finished tying her to the tree like a sacrificial lamb. The blackbirds cawed louder in thanks. Rachel closed her eyes.

"Come and feast," Justin shouted in to the air. "Come my-"

The words were cut short. Rachel waited for the sensation of birds eating her alive. Nothing came. She opened her eyes.

Nathan was on the floor, wrestling with the grisly spectre.

Her spirit soared, as the rain still poured down on her. Lightning lit up the scene in front of her.

"Who're you?" Justin growled, as he broke free. The flashes of light reflecting off his eye.

"I'm the one that should've been here last time. I don't have a clue what's going on, but I do know you're one ugly son of a bitch."

Justin twisted the stained blade in his hand. "Son-of-a-bitch. I'm going to gut you like a fish."

He lunged, but Nathan managed to twist his body out of the path of the knife. He lost his footing on the slippery, wet gravel. Justin was on top of him in a flash. He lifted Nathan's body in the air and tossed him against the beams holding up the porch.

Rachel heard the bones crack. But she didn't stop. She had been tugging at the ropes and she could feel them loosening. She was almost free.

A gust of wind howled past her. She turned her head away to shield her face from the pelting rain.

She stopped struggling.

David was standing in the window.

***

He didn't know why he went to the window first. David could feel the life draining from him. But he wanted to see her one more time. The woman that had changed his fate. If only he'd have been honest, he thought. If only he hadn't heard her soft, sweet sobs that day. Things could've been so different. He took one last look. It didn't matter now.

He thought about running. Leaving everyone and everything behind. Then he realised there was one fundamental flaw in his plan; the house would never let him go. Even if he did manage to get out, it wouldn't let him be. It would follow him, haunt him, until one day he would buy a gun and a bottle of liquor. His mind was already fractured with his schizophrenia. It was under control, but it had already started to spiral out of control since being back in town. It would only get worse. Well, Doctor David Cochrane, formerly Langrishe, would not live in fear.

He took one final look out of the window. The grim impersonation of his brother was wreathed in blackbirds. Rachel wasn't the only person to have suffered from the evil that infected the house. His own family had been torn apart, their reputation ripped asunder. It had gotten so bad that he had changed his surname, not wanting to be associated with his brother. He felt ashamed. His brother had died horrifically. David missed him so much. His fooling around, his love of life, his kind heart. Everything.

His numb limbs shuffled him towards the kitchen. The only sounds were his faint heartbeat and dripping droplets of blood on the hardwood floor. That'll stain, he thought with grim glee.

It didn't take long to find the heavy hammer and blow torch. He looked at the exposed pipes. He knew it wouldn't be easy. He knew the house would fight back. But he would do the job. By Christ, he would do the job.

"I'll be seeing you soon, bro," he whispered, bringing the hammer up above his head.

***

"No," Rachel said, as she saw where the birds were heading. She had pushed the image of David out of her mind, knowing he had to be dead already. It was delirium, she told herself. Just another ghost.

She watched the blackbirds swoop down and curve in an arc towards the house and then Justin. She knew where they were heading next.

"NATHAN, RUN!"

He had to have heard the words, but he just didn't move. Rachel's heart was racing. She pulled harder and harder at the ropes. The birds were everywhere pecking at her, their wings beating her.

Suffocating.

She had to get free. She could feel the birds tearing her apart. The ropes were biting in to her skin. The window shutters were going wild. She could hear them banging and crashing against the house.

There was black everywhere. She had no idea where Nathan was. Her energy was depleted. Any minute she would pass out.

Justin was on her in a second. Like Moses parting the Red Sea, he walked through them, not a single one touching him. His face was twisted out of shape. He no longer resembled her first love.

"So, sugar pie," he said, the words coming out in a hiss. "Ready to join me forever?"

"Screw you."

He laughed in her face, as he pulled the knife above his head. Lightning flashed.

Rachel prayed.

Justin stopped and spun to face the house. To face itself.

***

David could see them all. Justin, Chelsea, Tim. The McCain family was there. And of course Lilly. They all smiled encouragement. The smell of gas, spewing from the newly broken pipe, filled the room.

He smiled back.

His lifeless hand fell on the blowtorch.

It felt good.

CHAPTER TWENTY-THREE

The explosion shook the hillside like an angry god. Citizens of Willows Peak claimed the ball of fire that erupted into the night sky could be seen from all the way over the other side of town. It was the dreary eyed patrons of Logan's Bar, those that were always drunk and there until closing, that felt the blast. Whiskey bottles and beer glasses chinked together behind the bar. According to Gloria Bennett, owner and barmaid, the building shook so hard that a framed picture of Elvis jumped right off the wall and smashed on the floor. It was her favourite one.

According to the later reports, the quiet streets filled with people just standing and watching. Mrs Ryan, bed and breakfast proprietor, described how people came out of their homes, some fully clothed, others in nothing more than pyjamas and slippers. They exchanged glances with each other. At first it was fear and bewilderment, but then it felt like somebody slapped them, as a deep, easy sensation went through them. The faces turned to smiles. Everything was going to be okay. It felt good.

Mr Krupp, local businessman, was sitting in his car at the time. He had only just arrived home after being with his mistress. He was contemplating whether to leave his shrill bitch of a wife for good, when he saw the yellow tips of the flames burst skywards. It reminded him of the nuclear bomb test footage; the black mushroom cloud spiralling ever upwards.

Similar events happened all across town. The emergency

service switchboard was jammed, as panicked voices shrieked down the lines wanting answers. Some believed the damn commies had finally struck. Others thought aliens from distant planets were invading to enslave the populace. None would ever guess the truth...

Rachel wasn't aware of any of it until much later when she read it in the news. She had managed to free herself, just as the explosion hit. The force of it sent her reeling backwards, end over end like a Fourth of July Catherine Wheel flying through the air. She thought the heat would sear her skin off. She landed in a heap several feet away from the tree.

For several moments she just lay there, the rain hitting her face. Was she dead, she wondered? No, she was alive. Her heart thundered and her dislocated shoulder throbbed. If she was dead, she wouldn't feel a thing, she was sure of it.

Once the ringing in her ears had subsided, all she could hear was the distant rumbling of the storm fading away. There were no screams, no blackbirds and no maniacal laughter coming at her. There was nothing. Only peace. For the first time in as long as she could remember, the silence wasn't awkward, or oppressive. It was bliss.

She slowly sat up, her battered and bleeding body groaned under the exertion. Pushing the pain away, she opened her eyes.

The front corner of the house, what would have been the living room, was gone. It had been completely obliterated in the explosion. Flames leapt from the gaping hole, billowing black smoke into the sky. The smell of ash filled her nose. The house was quietly being consumed by fire. It was funny how often history repeats itself, she thought with grim amusement, remembering the first time she had witnessed the same sight. But what had caused it this time? She mused, unable to understand. Explosions like that didn't just happen. Something had to have caused it.

She rubbed her eyes, not trusting what she saw.

Lilly was standing in the upstairs window, looking down

at her. The young girl smiled and raised her hand in a gesture of goodbye. Behind her were more faces from the past. Chelsea had her arm around Tim, the familiar longing on her face as she smiled at him. Justin was there too, goofing around with his brother. They all looked out at her, a faint glimmer of approval filling the dark window. Rachel nodded back at them. She understood.

The vision of David in the living room window hadn't been caused by delirium at all. It had been real. He had caused the explosion. Rachel didn't know how, but she knew it was him. A tear slid down her cheek. He had died saving them.

Faint groaning to her left caught her attention. Nathan. She had totally forgotten that he was there with her.

She scrambled along the gravel towards him, on her hands and knees, not ready to try standing yet.

"Nathan, can you hear me?" she asked, cradling his head in her lap.

He was in a state. His clothes were torn, his skin ripped to shreds in places, a huge gash above his left eye. But he was breathing.

"Come on, Nate. You've got to wake up."

Nothing.

"Please Nathan, I need you." Tears began to fall more rapidly, splashing down on his forehead. "I can't lose you too."

His eyes flickered open. "Hey pretty lady. I ain't going anywhere."

Rachel didn't know whether to laugh, or continue crying. She decided she could do both, as she bent over and hugged him. They embraced for several minutes before she let go.

Nathan looked at her. "Is he…?"

"He's gone. Dead, along with the house. It was the only thing keeping him around."

"And the birds?"

Rachel looked around, her brow furrowing deeper and deeper. There were no blackbirds circling overhead and no bodies littering the ground. The embodiment of the house had called them his children. Had they been connected to the house too?

She looked down on her friend with a smile. "They're gone."

"All of them?"

"Every single one."

Nathan looked puzzled. "I don't understand it, Rach. H-how was Justin alive?"

She looked up at the house, her eyes gazing in to the distance. The flames danced in them. "They were all here. They were always here."

"Oh," he replied, letting the night grow silent around them.

Then, they waited.

***

A long time after that, the fire department, along with the sheriff, arrived. They just sat there in silence, watching the house collapse in on itself, the fire eating away at the old wooden beams. Nathan sat up on his own, wincing every now and then with the pain. Rachel heard the blaring sirens getting closer, long before the red trucks crested the hill. She ignored the firemen, as they went about the dangerous business of putting out the fire.

Paramedics charged towards them. They asked questions like, *are you hurt? Where is the pain? Can you move?* She gave them simple answers, her eyes fixed on the burning timbers. She felt numb. The shock settling in no doubt, she thought. Was it truly over? A part of her believed she could have her life back. But another part, one much bigger, doubted it.

A familiar voice broke her out of her melancholy.

"Rachel, Nathan, thank God you're okay," Becky said, dashing towards them. She flung her arms around Nathan, almost bowling him over.

"Hey, easy there girl," he replied, hugging her back. "I don't know about okay, but we're alive."

Rachel said nothing. They would be okay. She wasn't so sure about herself.

"What the hell happened?" Becky asked. "Where's David?"

"It's a long story," Rachel replied.

She noticed her two friends exchange worried glances, but neither said anything. The paramedics led her towards an ambulance, informing her that the doctors at the hospital would want to give her the once over. Most of the words went in one ear and out of the other.

As they got closer, she noticed Sheriff Ross waiting there.

"Don't go disappearin' anywhere, Miss James," he said, fixing his eyes on her. "We're goin' to want some answers from you."

Rachel nodded and climbed in to the back. Becky sat next to her, taking hold of her hand. It was small comfort. She could see Nathan exchanging heated words with the sheriff, but couldn't hear them. He climbed in and the paramedic slammed the door shut.

Within seconds they were speeding down the drive, the gravel crunching beneath the heavy black tyres. She stared out of the small window in silence. The house shrunk to a tiny dot as they moved away. The locket around her neck felt cold.

To my high-school sweet heart: Always and Forever.

She would be able to see the orange smudge on the horizon from the hospital, the flames burning all night long. It wouldn't be until sleep caught up with her that she could forget.

But even then it stood, forever in her mind.

The house of wood.

Epilogue

Cold winter winds whipped up around the hillside, dashing through the lifeless branches of the woodlands. Grey, forlorn clouds swept across the sky, casting long shadows over the desolate town. The sun hardly ever shone anymore. Or that's what the people had come to believe. Too much had happened.

Too much that couldn't be explained.

The sounds of crunching under heavy feet filtered up into the cold air, as a female made her way up the winding path. The remains of a house sat on top of the hill. When asked about it later, people would have sworn that you could still smell the woodburning. It was the last time she ever wanted to come back here. She didn't want to ever see it again. But she had to make sure it was still gone.

As Rachel crested the top of the hill, the burnt out structure came into full view, the charred, wooden timbers reaching out towards the sky like bones in a grave. She bowed her head and thanked the Lord no one had rebuilt it.

The place had taken away everything from her: her home, her friends, it had even almost taken her life. There was an evil here. A darkness that had plagued the nearby town for too long. She couldn't feel it anymore, but something inside her wondered if it was over. A part of her wondered if it would ever be over.

She made her way towards the only tree that would have made up the garden of the house. It stood there, alone and untouched by fire. A child's swing hung lifeless on one of the branches, lacking a child to play with it. Next to the tree was the object she had come to see. A small gravestone with a single word on it. Lilly.

Rachel knelt down at the foot of the tombstone. She placed a single red rose in front of it.

"Thank you for saving my life, Lilly," she said, resting her hand on the weathered stone surface. "If it hadn't been for you, I would've died here just like all the others. You watched over this place for all those years, trying as hard as you could to protect anybody stupid enough to come up here." A single tear dripped down the lines of her face. She had decided to do this a long time ago; during all the sleepless nights she had spent at the asylum. No one believed her. Of course, Nathan tried to defend her corner, but he had his own problems to deal with. Even he had left town now, to start a new life somewhere else. There was nothing left here except the stale smell of death. "Well you can rest now. There's someone else that can do this for you."

Rachel stood up, her eyes fixed on the burnt out structure. Even though it was completely gutted, it still loomed large and foreboding. She'd never let anybody suffer like she had.

Her right hand reached around to the back pocket of her black denim jeans. Her other hand clutched at a locket. She pulled out a handgun, softly cocking the trigger, as she raised it to her temple. This was it. There was no doubting, no fear, no ties to hold her back. We're all ghosts waiting to die, she thought, as her finger tightened.

Townsfolk would later claim that a clear shot rang out over the hillside at around four o'clock in the afternoon, only a few hours after she had served her time and was released from the state psychiatric hospital.

After the sound dispersed, the swing slowly rocked back and forth. In the distance, five blackbirds soared across the sky.

ACKNOWLEDGEMENT

Firstly, I'd like to thank all the avid readers that bought the first edition of this book, for not only believing in me as a writer, but for having as much faith in this book as I do. Another thank you must go to Murray Eckett, who helped me whip the text into shape once more. I'd also like to thank Carl Muddiman for sacrificing his hands taking my superfast dictation. I'll make sure that I go slower next time. A big thank you has to go to my granddad, without whose love and support I never would have achieved my MA in Creative Writing, which sowed the seeds for this novel. And to my sister, Stacey, whose opinion I'll always seek out first when it comes to editing. But the biggest thank you has to go to my parents who raised me to think big and to never let any obstacle stand in my way. Without your love, I wouldn't be around today. Finally, thank you to everyone that buys this book. Without you, I wouldn't have a job.

ABOUT THE AUTHOR

Anthony Price

Anthony Price is a thirty-six year old male residing in the UK, in Canterbury. An avid reader and film fanatic and having always wanted to be a writer, he was first published at age fifteen and since achieving his MA in Creative Writing, has had several short stories published in e-zines and anthologies.

His first novel, The House of Wood, had been in the works for three years and started off as a small writing exercise on his MA. Being a disabled writer, he has had his fair share of doubters, so this novel is extra special. It's available in paperback via Amazon and e-book format at all other retailers.

He's also the author of his own horror anthology titled, Tales of Merryville, which is available to buy in e-book format on Amazon. His second novel, Vigilante Chronicles Book One: High Voltage, was a change of direction and genre. It's available In paperback on Amazon.

Anthony is currently working on several creative projects to look out for in the future, including more horror novels, a feature film and a TV show.

You can follow him on all social media platforms:

Facebook - https://www.facebook.com/anthonyjpricepage

Twitter - https://twitter.com/AJPrice_Author

Printed in Great Britain
by Amazon